"Skylar?" he murmured huskily. "You still with me?"

Oh, hell. Her eyes flashed open. So did her jaw. Of course her hope that Zane wouldn't remember her would be futile. He probably had one of those eidetic memories with every minuscule detail of his life stored inside his annoyingly intelligent brain.

"What, did you think I didn't recognize you?" His smile widened. "Of course I recognized you..."

He raked his gaze down her yet again—taking in the delicate ribbon straps at the base of her neck. The halter-neck style meant she was unable to wear a bra beneath it—though to be fair she didn't really need a bra. But as his gaze swept down her, she felt her breasts respond again as if his glance were actually a stroke. Infuriated with herself, she willed her gaze to be more of a slap back. But when he lifted his focus back to her eyes, his smile merely widened from smirk to blindingly gorgeous.

"Just as you recognize me," he added.

Billion-Dollar Bet

*Three rival billionaires... Two huge problems...
One bet to solve them both!*

Zane deMarco, Adam Courtney and Cade Landry
have two problems:

1. In their individual and ruthless pursuits of a failing
company, they're pushing the share price sky-high.

2. The billionaire playboys are being scandalously
called out online for their dating habits.

There's only one way to solve both. Whoever can
stay a one-woman man for the entire summer will
not only rid themselves of the rumors but add the
company to their business portfolio.

They have a lot to lose, but a lot to gain. And what's
betting all of them also find passion worth risking it
all for?

Read Zane's story in:
Billion-Dollar Dating Game by Natalie Anderson

Available now!

Look out for Adam's story:
Boss with Benefits
by Lucy King

And Cade's story
by Heidi Rice

Both coming soon!

BILLION-DOLLAR DATING GAME

NATALIE ANDERSON

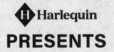

H Harlequin

PRESENTS

Harlequin® PRESENTS™

Recycling programs for this product may not exist in your area.

ISBN-13: 978-1-335-93909-8

Billion-Dollar Dating Game

Copyright © 2024 by Natalie Anderson

 Harlequin Enterprises ULC
22 Adelaide St. West, 41st Floor
Toronto, Ontario M5H 4E3, Canada
www.Harlequin.com

Printed in Lithuania

MIX
Paper | Supporting responsible forestry
FSC® C021394

USA TODAY bestselling author **Natalie Anderson** writes emotional contemporary romance full of sparkling banter, sizzling heat and uplifting endings—perfect for readers who love to escape with empowered heroines and arrogant alphas who are too sexy for their own good. When she's not writing, you'll find Natalie wrangling her four children, three cats, two goldfish and one dog...and snuggled in a heap on the sofa with her husband at the end of the day. Follow her at natalie-anderson.com.

Books by Natalie Anderson

Harlequin Presents

The Night the King Claimed Her
The Boss's Stolen Bride
My One-Night Heir

Innocent Royal Runaways

Impossible Heir for the King
Back to Claim His Crown

Billion-Dollar Christmas Confessions

Carrying Her Boss's Christmas Baby

Jet-Set Billionaires

Revealing Her Nine-Month Secret

Visit the Author Profile page
at Harlequin.com for more titles.

CHAPTER ONE

ZANE DEMARCO INHALED DEEP, stretched out long, and let the sauna's dry heat sharpen every sense. Their squash score was still a three-way tie after nine rounds and while they could go all day, it would make little difference.

'Are you going to reveal why you summoned us here at the crack of dawn on a holiday?' he asked the brooding man sitting along from him. 'Because if it was to break the tie and take the lead, that plan sure as hell backfired.'

Adam Courtney shot him a withering glance. Zane just grinned back. His old rowing rival from his brief university stint in the UK was as laser focused and hyper-competitive as ever. The fact that wild card Cade Landry had also shown his face so early in the day underscored the significance of their meeting. While he sometimes came to their eternally equal squash sessions, the lone wolf didn't stick round for any bro banter. But Zane knew why he'd lingered today. They *all* knew the reason. But he prompted Adam into the conversation anyway.

Adam pushed a button on the infrared sauna and sent the temperature soaring before answering. 'Helberg Holdings.'

Bingo.

Helberg Holdings was an old money conglomerate—media, jewellery, retail property, hotels, everything imaginable, and—frankly because of that overreach—down on its luck. Reed Helberg, the last of the Helberg dynasty, had died seven months ago, and without its formidable, all-controlling head, the entity was now vulnerable. If changes weren't made soon, the entire operation could implode and leave little to salvage. The best option was to break it apart and sell off the bits that still worked. Corporate raiders often got a bad rap, but Zane had overseen many successful rebuilds from the parts of previous companies hc'd bought and broken up. And yes, he'd made plenty of money doing it. But this time was different. This time was personal.

'What about it?' Zane stretched lazily.

'You and Cade have both been buying up shares,' Adam gritted out.

'Him too?' Zane nodded towards Cade, who was taking his time to join them.

'Yes.'

Ah well, the game was afoot. But because of Reed Helberg, Zane had spent years literally broken. So Zane would be the one to break Reed's most treasured thing. That was fair, right?

But now he merely shrugged as Cade settled into the corner seat of the sauna. 'Well, it's highly leveraged, vulnerable and has lots of assets… What's not to like?'

Adam's gaze narrowed. 'An overinflated purchase price.'

'Scared it's gonna get too much for you?' Zane countered dryly.

Actually, that *was* a potential problem. Too many interested buyers meant trouble. Cade remained silent, but Zane noticed the loner's gaze briefly drop to the scars zigzagging up Zane's thigh. Zane stayed sprawled back and refused to cover the unsightly purple streaks. People saw damage and assumed weakness. They were wrong. Where there were scars, there was strength.

'I need you both to back off,' Adam said.

A frigid edge sliced into the sweltering atmosphere.

Zane didn't do deals with guys like Adam or Cade. They were too alike, too alone, frankly too obstinate. So they fished in their own ponds and kept their battles to the squash court. It was safest for everyone that way.

'Helberg?' A muscle in Cade's jaw flicked. 'Not happening…'

Zane slowly shook his head and shot Adam a mock sad expression. 'No can do.'

Helberg's destruction was his alone to enjoy and he would do whatever it took to eliminate the competition. But these two were sharp and he'd have to think creatively through this one.

'It's a once-in-a-lifetime opportunity, y'all,' Cade said.

No shit. Any other company and Zane might consider walking away, but Reed Helberg was the whole reason why Zane had scars on his skin and metal pinning his bones beneath it. Zane was going to enjoy ripping apart the thing Reed had been so vainglorious about. The thing he'd never thought Zane was good enough for. Carve and cull was the only way through.

Adam inhaled deeply. 'Then we have a problem.'

'Actually, we have *problems*. Plural.' Cade glowered from his corner.

'What the hell are you talking about?' Adam's frown mushroomed.

Cade stiffened. 'Clearly you don't read *Blush*.'

'The women's glamour magazine?' Adam asked incredulously. 'You read that?'

'No, I don't read it, but my PR consultant does. He just

texted me,' Cade growled. 'Did y'all know we are the star players in their latest dumb article: "The Billionaire Bachelors Least Likely to Marry"? Apparently, we three have been tagged as the One-Date Wonders…the guys with the longest odds, and they've already started a tally on how many dates we'll have racked up by Labour Day.'

The *what*? Zane cocked his head, both disbelieving of and bamboozled by this unexpected diversion. 'You're kidding.'

Privacy wasn't assured once your bank balance hit a certain threshold, so yeah, sometimes they were on those tragic 'youngest billionaires' lists and occasionally some appalling clickbait list involving paparazzi pictures of them poolside, but this one was even more ick. 'Who I date is no one's business but mine.' Zane shook his head, brushing it off. 'And I'm not going to stop—' He was happily married to his work, thanks very much. And very happy to play the little time he took away from it. Work hard, play hard—balance was best, after all. '—I've no plans to settle down. Ever.'

'Neither do I,' Adam snapped.

Zane blinked at the identical frowns deepening on Adam's and Cade's faces. The intensity was interesting. And possibly useful.

'They're turning our sex lives into a joke,' Cade added after a moment. 'And getting a lot of traction. And that's not the kind of media attention I want for my business. Do you?'

Zane didn't give a damn if people were so bored they wanted to bash his private life for their own amusement, but it clearly bothered both Cade and Adam.

'Exactly how much traction are we talking about?' Zane drawled.

Cade tensed even more. 'The hashtag "onedatewonders" is the top trending topic in the US on most of the main apps today. That much traction. And just about every American female online seems to have an opinion now about our sex lives… We're basically the red meat at the centre of a social media feeding frenzy.'

Adam winced.

Yeah, *#onedatewonders* was a truly appalling hashtag.

'My PR team is freaking out about it,' Cade added. 'Personally, I don't give a damn what a bunch of clickbait junkies and their enablers think of my dating habits…but no way in hell am I letting anyone make me look like a jerk who can't keep his junk in his pants.'

'We need to find a way to shut it down,' Adam muttered grimly.

Zane rubbed his hand along his jaw and considered the reactions of his rivals. Despite his protests, this article had obviously hit Cade on a visceral level, and Adam looked even moodier than usual. People made mistakes when they were emotional and both these guys were zooming towards anger and outrage.

Zane didn't become intensely emotional about anything. On the rare occasion something slipped beneath his skin, he swiftly suppressed it, because after his father had walked out he'd had to 'stay strong.' After he'd realised his exhausted mother was struggling and secretly wanted him gone too, he'd learned not to 'be a bother.' When he was housebound recuperating for years he'd had to 'be quiet' so his overworked mother could rest…

He didn't show hurt, didn't cry, didn't complain. When Reed Helberg had humiliated him more than once, he hadn't so much as winced. Hell, when the first girl he'd fancied had hung him out to dry in front of her overly controlling father, he'd hid how stupidly much *that* had hurt him. And he'd vowed not to let *anyone* hurt him ever again. And besides all that, he'd spent years suppressing *physical* pain, which was a far tougher task than swallowing the mild embarrassment from this little internet flurry.

But perhaps he could direct Adam and Cade's obvious discomfort to his own advantage. Indeed, the answer to the magazine slur was obvious to him. If they weren't seen out with a series of women, then there would be no stupid tally and nothing for the trash columnists to report on. The question was whether Cade and Adam could cope with that constraint—was that, in fact, a prospect for a competition?

Zane deMarco thrived on competition. The tougher the better. It made winning all the sweeter.

'What if we take ourselves off the market?' he mused.

'Forget it.' Cade sounded horrified. 'No way am I *actually* getting hitched to shut this down.'

'Absolutely not.' Adam was even more appalled. 'It's out of the question.'

Zane bit back a chuckle. Yeah, both of them were too volatile and that was good. 'Did I say anything about getting hitched?' he countered, oh-so-mildly. 'This is a countdown, right? So why don't we stop the clock before it even starts. All we have to do is each date one woman—and one woman only—from now until Labour Day. Simple.'

Cade's jaw dropped. 'You're kidding. You actually want to pander to this garbage?'

'Not particularly, but I'm betting you two will break long before I do.' Zane watched them closely.

Cade's blue eyes glinted. 'I'll take that bet, because the last time I looked, you're a bigger serial dater than the both of us.'

Usually true, but also irrelevant. While generally sex

was a healthy part of his life, more than half of his most recent dates had ended early and chastely. He was tired of the more-than-sexual expectations he didn't have the capacity to fulfil. But Zane would endure anything to get hold of this company, and what was a little discomfort or deprivation? He'd suffered far worse pain than having to sleep with just the one woman for a while. Besides which, it was only dating her, right? Not necessarily anything more.

'You don't even know what the stakes are.' Adam shot Cade an astounded look.

Zane let the moment hang. He liked playing all kinds of games because his favourite thing in the world was to *win*, and because he'd come from having nothing for so long, he'd never been afraid of going all in. His risks had paid off.

'My Helberg shares,' he said softly and watched them both stiffen.

Uh-huh. That had their attention. His amusement rippled across his face but beneath that facade he tensed. Winning Helberg Holdings was non-negotiable.

'Hold on a minute.' Cade leaned forward, frowning. 'You'd bet on Helberg? Are you serious?'

Deadly, actually. But he played up his carelessness. 'Sure. Why not?'

If Cade and Adam thought he wasn't all that serious, they wouldn't take him as a serious threat. He'd lull them, then strike. 'It's Independence Day today. What if we meet back here on Labour Day. Winner takes all accumulated shares and has an unimpeded run at Helberg.'

That gave them a couple of months. There was no way either Adam or Cade would date only one woman for all that time. Both were allergic to relationships, both exuded intensity and drive and both did not like being told what they could and couldn't do by anyone. Put people under pressure and they made mistakes. Meanwhile, it would give Zane room to finish his due diligence and finalise divestment plans for Helberg. Plus if they all backed off for now, it would hopefully stop the share price surge.

'Have you completely lost your mind?' Adam shook his head.

Zane shrugged. He enjoyed doing the absolute opposite of what anyone expected of him. It made a challenge all the sweeter when he succeeded.

'This *Blush* business is an annoyance, but I'm more interested in sorting out which of us gets Helberg. This is a good way to take you guys on and beat you both for once and all. Two birds, one stone.'

'It's nuts…' Cade stared at him. 'But it also makes sense.'

'It's ridiculous,' Adam shot them down crisply. 'Not only will it not work, it's also immoral. And think of the unwitting women we'd be dragging into it. Where's your integrity?'

Zane bit back a laugh. Apparently perfectly posh Englishman Adam was too straitlaced to think creatively. As far as Zane was concerned, there was no reason why the woman he chose to date for the duration should be either unwitting or indeed unwilling. Everything—indeed, every*one*—had a price. All he had to do was find a woman savvy enough to take the deal he was going to discreetly offer her. But Zane was hardly about to point that option out to all-but-aristocratic Adam.

Zane had hauled his way to the top of his particular tree all by himself—he'd had no family money, no hand-outs from anyone else, least of all old man Helberg. He'd done everything on his own and he always would. Taking Helberg apart piece by tarnished piece all by himself would be particularly satisfying.

'You got a better idea?' He let a sprinkle of saltiness out. 'Because the likelihood of us stepping out of each other's way just because you asked nicely is…*what*?'

Cade's rare low laugh sounded. 'Afraid you'll lose, Courtney?'

Adam dated the least of the three of them. Cade, on the other hand, was barely tamed, while Zane knew his own reputation was voracious, which meant—once he'd thought about it—Adam would believe he would win this thing. Easily.

Sure enough, a split second later Adam nodded. 'Not at all… Quite the opposite…'

Yeah, it seemed Adam had mentally resolved his own integrity issue, while Cade simply looked wolfishly determined. Fortunately, Zane was heading home this afternoon and there'd be zero chance of encountering temptation there. After a courtesy drop-in to his neighbour's Independence Day party, he'd take the rest of the weekend to consider who he was going to approach and how.

'So just to clarify,' Adam added stiffly. 'We date one woman each between now and Labour Day. Anyone caught dating more than one woman in that time relinquishes their claim on Helberg.'

'Right.' Zane nodded. 'I'm in.'

'You're on,' Cade agreed.

Adam sighed as he rolled his eyes. 'May the best man win…'

Zane smiled. The best man absolutely would.

CHAPTER TWO

THREE BLUE-EYED BILLIONAIRE bachelors walked into a health club...

Sounded like the start of a bad joke, right? Or a dream opportunity for someone inspired by *Blush* magazine's latest article questioning whether there was a woman alive who could secure more than one date with any of them. The One-Date Wonders themselves: Adam Courtney. Cade Landry. Zane deMarco.

For Skylar Bennet, it was neither funny nor a dream. It was a full-fledged nightmare. She froze in the cafe across the street, staring in horrified amazement as, within the space of two minutes, the three subjects of the tasteless article currently being quoted all over social media stalked in. Well, Adam and Cade stalked. Zane simply sauntered.

Typical.

Skylar drained her coffee and ordered another. She'd done her run and didn't have to get to the office immediately, so she'd wait to see them walk out again. It wasn't the first time she'd watched out a window hoping to see Zane deMarco, but she wasn't some tragic teen suffering from her first crush now.

It was Saturday—the Fourth of July in fact, so it was a long weekend as well, but those guys didn't holiday like normal people. They weren't rolling up to a gym for fun and fitness. Setting up deals was their sport and recreation because nothing mattered more to them than making money. But as much as these three had in common, it wasn't normal to see them *together*. They were *rivals*, not besties.

Maybe that article did have something to do with it. As gross as it was, it was also accurate—they were each ridiculously young to have achieved billionaire status and all those pictures proved they were unrepentantly active on the social scene. But she didn't know much about Adam and Cade other than what else had been written—British Adam was all aristocratic old money, while Cade had built his construction company into a billionaire business. But she knew more than enough about Zane deMarco. The man was avaricious and an annihilator and he did not give a damn about what anyone thought of him. Which is why Skylar was quite sure it wasn't that article drawing them together today—it was something far worse.

They were coming for Helberg Holdings. That company was more than her place of employment; it had changed her life. She'd been a beneficiary of the Helberg Foundation—awarded scholarships first for senior high school, then a full ride for her entire degree. She'd interned for them through her summer breaks and come to work fulltime in the company headquarters here in Manhattan as soon as she'd graduated.

It was the plan her father had dreamed she'd follow—to be the first in her class, the first in his family to get a degree, to work in the city in a prestigious firm, to *excel*, and to show loyalty… The Helberg scholarships had enabled her to do exactly that.

She'd owed. She still did. Now, years later, she'd made her way onto the HR team, but since the untimely death of the CEO Reed Helberg seven months ago, whispers about a takeover had been growing. The optimists in the office wanted it to be bought by someone who'd restore the conglomerate to its former glory, but Skylar was afraid it would be ripped apart by some ruthless corporate raider.

Someone like Zane deMarco.

The jerk scooped up vulnerable companies, stripped and sold their assets and ditched the rest. He had zero commitment. Which was exactly how he approached women as well—absolutely a 'one-date wonder,' he'd accumulated as many notches on his bedpost as he had dollars in the bank. But while he was all fun and charm on the outside, Skylar knew the truth. He didn't just have the arrogance of the successful—he was a *soulless* vessel who lived only to make cold, hard cash. He didn't truly care about anything—other than getting further along an endless path of acquisition and excess. In short, Skylar hated him. She had for years now.

It didn't help that he could kiss a woman like no one else. That once, so very briefly, almost a decade ago, *she'd* been his target. She'd fallen for his looks, his superficial charm… Fortunately, her father had intervened before she'd foolishly given Zane everything he'd wanted—the way so many others had since.

And of course he'd forgotten her and moved on to his next target—the same way he had with all the companies he'd shredded and the employees he'd left redundant. They couldn't be more different.

The irony was that they'd come from similar backgrounds. They'd lived in the same run-down apartment building in one of the few affordable housing complexes in Belhaven Bay, a picturesque village in the Hamptons, when they were kids. Sounded fancy, right? Wrong.

Growing up in one of the most famous and wealthiest areas in the world ought to be wonderful, but being a year-rounder was a vastly different experience to being a child of the rich and famous who dropped in only for weekends of the best weather. She and Zane had other things in common too—they'd both been raised by a single parent: Skylar by her dad, a caretaker, and Zane by his mum, a cleaner. They'd even gone to the same school until she'd won that scholarship to that boarding school upstate for her senior years. And unfortunately, she still remembered the quiet boy he'd been so very long ago. He'd found her not long after her mother had run off with another man. A few days later, a disbelieving Skylar had tried to find her—a naïve, heartbroken kid wandering down the road with no direction or plan. Zane had come across her a couple blocks over from their complex. She'd been crying—as pitiful as she'd been hopeful. He'd not said anything. He'd just taken a bit of raspberry candy from a packet in his pocket and handed it to her. He'd waited while she'd eaten it. While she'd calmed down. Then he'd walked her back to their building, up the stairs, and left her at her door. They'd been *children* but he'd been her friend. Just for that moment. Because he'd roamed freely as a kid—some would say wildly—while his mother worked long hours. But from then on, Skylar had stayed inside, obeying her father's new rules.

Because she'd needed to be safe and he'd needed to know where she was at all times. She'd needed to be good and quiet and study hard. And she had. Because she'd not wanted her dad to disappear on her too.

Then Zane and his mother had been in an accident. He'd had to take a long time off school and hadn't roamed their block any more, and she'd hardly seen him at all.

It wasn't until the summer after her first year at that

boarding school when everything had changed. She'd been sixteen. Still processing her mother's absence, still pleasing her father—adhering to his strict lessons on loyalty and work ethic and not succumbing to distractions. She'd watched the world from the balcony as she'd studied. From her bedroom window in the evenings as she'd combed her hair. Late one night, she'd spotted Zane in the darkness across the courtyard. He'd been on the balcony of the two-bedroom unit that was a mirror of her own. He'd become something of a local legend by then—his jaw-droppingly elite academic performance overshadowed by rumours of some online financial success. But that night he'd looked moody and serious and honestly as lonely as she'd felt for years. He'd been wearing nothing but an old pair of shorts and unfortunately for her, in the shadow and gleam of that moonlit night he'd had the beauty of a brooding angel— tousled coal-coloured hair, sharp cheekbones, a sculpted torso. He'd leaned out with his arms wide on the railing and stared down at the courtyard as if he were Atlas himself with the world on his shoulders. Her heart hadn't just thumped painfully, it had flipped right over. She'd stepped back into the darkness of her own room but kept watching him for the full fifty minutes he was out there, and at one point he'd looked up, staring directly at her window, and even though it'd been dark and she'd known there was no way he could have seen her, she'd flushed.

From that night on she'd ached to see more of him— naively imagining they were kindred spirits, what with all those commonalities—and more of him she had then seen. It had become her habit to go for a run early in the mornings—not that she'd been good at it, but it'd been the one way of getting out that her father had allowed. She'd argued she needed to be fit to study well. To her surprise—and secret pleasure—she'd passed Zane on her way out a couple of times. He'd smiled at her. He had a captivating smile.

Then, on one of her last days home, as she'd come back from her run, she'd all but slammed into him as she'd turned into the stairwell on her side of the building. He'd steadied her and in the cool shade he'd smiled and his pale blue eyes had gleamed, and she'd felt energy emanating from him. Later, she'd learned it was around this time that he'd made his first million. All but overnight, so the story went. As a freaking teenager. Now she realised he'd wanted to celebrate in true playboy fashion—with a female conquest. A notch for his new belt. But back then, she'd thought his piercingly pale blue eyes had seen straight to her soul. Or at least, he'd noticed the movement of her mouth.

'What are you eating?' he'd asked.

It had been raspberry candy, of course. Her favourite and always her post-run self-reward.

'Got any to share?' he'd asked when she'd told him.

She'd shaken her head as she'd swallowed. 'That was my last piece.'

'Yeah?' he'd muttered huskily. 'Maybe I can still have a little taste.'

With that, he'd made his move. The kiss had been tentative at first. Soft. Gentle. Then it just changed. *She'd* changed. It was like a wildfire had exploded within her. She'd moaned, suddenly all the more breathless. She'd become so hot, so malleable in his arms. She'd have let him do anything. So *easy*. He'd lifted her up, surprising her with his strength as he'd pressed her against the wall with his lean body. But *she'd* been the one to curl her leg around his slim hips, welcoming him closer. She'd been the one to hold him *so* tightly, recklessly racing with him towards the precipice of something she hadn't understood but innately knew would be profound. She'd lost all track of time. Of everything. All she'd known was that she'd wanted that contact more than anything.

So she hadn't heard the heavy tread of her father coming down the stairs. She hadn't stopped kissing Zane back, clutching him closer, letting him touch—

For a time after, she'd tried to reassure herself that it would have looked worse than it actually was—after all, she'd already been flushed and breathless and sweaty from her run—but being caught pinned against the wall by a panting Zane, her father had thought her disarray was because Zane had manhandled her...

The scalding mortification of that moment still overcame her even now, years later. Even though her father was no longer alive.

'Get off her!'

She'd been paralysed. Her father had pulled Zane back and shoved him from her. She'd slithered to the ground and said nothing to either her father or Zane as her father had suggested...assumed...*accused*.

She'd sunk back against that wall and watched the glittering passion in Zane's eyes morph into bitterness as she stayed silent in the face of her father's fury. And then even that bitterness had faded until he'd stood there, coolly and dispassionately enduring the endless onslaught of her father's rage.

'I don't care what money you've supposedly made. *Don't you dare* touch *my* daughter! *Don't you dare* help yourself—you'll never be good enough for her. You're a troublemaker, stay away!' Her father had berated him repeatedly before whirling to her. 'And *you*, get upstairs. *Don't you dare* squander the opportunities you've been given! *Don't you dare* ruin your future!'

He'd gone on and on and on. She'd been too stunned—too scared—too shamed to speak. She'd scuttled upstairs and hadn't dared leave the apartment again. Fortunately, it was only a few days before she'd had to return to school. She'd done so quietly and dutifully, repeatedly apologising to her still-disappointed father.

When he'd calmed down, when she'd finally summoned the courage, she tried to assure him Zane hadn't taken liberties, that she'd welcomed that kiss. But she hadn't said that right at the time.

And then her father had got angrier. *'Don't you dare let lust control you; don't you dare waste what you have on a boy who wants only one thing...'* It would, he'd lectured her, only lead her off the path into selfishness, into shirking responsibility. Disloyalty. After all, look at her mother—wasn't she the prime example of that?

Skylar had been devastated. She'd promised not to lose focus. She'd promised to make him proud again. There would be no boys—no lust. Not for years. Not—she hadn't realised at the time—really ever again.

When she'd returned the next holidays, Zane had left town and so had his mother, and a different family had lived in their apartment. She'd been glad. She'd tried hard not to follow word of Zane's success but it had been hard to avoid. He was the town's poster child. She'd seen the write-ups of the 'wunderkind' investor, seen the pictures of him at parties over in the UK even—always with a beautiful woman on his arm.

And the year after that she'd met him again. They'd both been guests at a formal graduation function of their old school. Even at eighteen she'd still felt awkward, wearing a thrift shop dress that was too big in the bust. Most dresses were still too big in the bust. She'd been nervously excited, knowing Zane was going to be there. Because despite everything, she'd never forgotten that kiss and at that point she'd not yet had another. At first she'd been too shy to look him in the eye; she'd forced her attention on being polite to Reed Helberg. The generous, old CEO rarely made appearances at events like that.

When she'd finally summoned the courage to glance over at Zane, he'd met her gaze for less than a second before coldly turning his back. She'd been flattened. He didn't talk directly to her. She'd noticed he'd not even politely applauded when she was announced as the Helberg Scholar—with a full ride to a prestigious university. He'd only deigned to shoot her a patronisingly sarcastic look as she'd sat back down, as if it were somehow disappointing to him that she'd accepted such an amazing offer. Anger had brewed in her then. But Zane hadn't bothered to look her way again. He'd spoken only briefly to Reed—and it was evident Zane hadn't thought much of him either. He'd been so rude he'd actually left before dessert, and on his way out he'd muttered to her beneath his breath.

'You're pathetic.'

His dismissal that night, his arrogant rudeness, had destroyed the remnants of her crush completely.

So, if she were an awful person, she'd whip out her phone right now and post an anonymous tip on social media to let the single women of the world know exactly where the three billionaire baits could be found. By now they were probably in the sauna—as if it wasn't hot enough in Manhattan in July. But these men did everything to extremes, including how many women they dated.

Skylar had zero interest in securing a date with any of them, least of all Zane deMarco. She only wanted to know whether he was discussing Helberg Holdings with those other sharks, but short of sneaking into the gym changing rooms to eavesdrop she wasn't about to find out. But she was certain Zane would want Helberg—it was exactly the kind of prize that he liked. Big and sparkling, coveted by all. He liked to take such things and tear them apart. Just because he could.

But if Zane ripped Helberg to bits, as she knew he would, he'd ruin the hopes and futures of countless other kids like her who would benefit from a Helberg scholarship. Plus he'd also threaten the livelihoods of so many workers who'd been loyal to Helberg for decades, and Skylar simply couldn't stand for that.

A bunch of people dressed in red, white and blue burst into the cafe, wreathed in smiles and excitement. Skylar stilled, remembering how the rest of the country wasn't working today because they had feasts and parties to attend with family and friends.

Zane deMarco might not have much family but he liked to party harder than anyone—especially with all his female 'friends.'

She pulled out her phone and did a quick search to remind herself that indeed this was the one time of year that he sometimes returned—not to the enclave of groundskeepers, caretakers, cleaners and cooks, but to an elite annual party at an oceanfront summer residence that would be a permanent palace for anyone ordinary. Danielle Chapman's Independence Day party.

Skylar jumped off her seat, energy bursting as a plan formed. A year older than her, it had been Danielle's job to settle Skylar into that new school because she spent part of her summers on Long Island. Despite their vast differences, they'd actually got on well and Danielle's approval had spared Skylar from a lot of bullying. Danielle still spent every summer on the island. Her parties were exclusive and discreet. The few invitations she sent were coveted, but every year she sent Skylar one—ditto to her Halloween party upstate. It was a running joke between them that Skylar could never make either because of work. Danielle had been teasing Skylar about working too hard for years. But Skylar wasn't a party person and to tell the truth, seeing via socials that Zane had attended Danielle's most recent parties, she'd had all the more reason *not* to go. Not this year though.

Skylar shot the health club doors a final glance. She wasn't going to sit around waiting just to spot them in the distance and do nothing. She had to take *action*. She'd *go* to Danielle's party tonight. Zane would surely be there and the guy was *not* discreet. If she could get within earshot, it might give her a chance to find out for herself what his plans were. She whipped out her phone while she still had momentum.

'You're coming?' Danielle shrieked less than a minute later. 'Fantastic! You know the dress code is white—do you need something to wear? You'll stay the night out here? Do you need transport?'

Skylar laughed as she refused all Danielle's offers of additional help. It was enough for her to actually go; she liked her independence. And she held back from asking for confirmation that Zane would be there. It was a crazy long shot, but one she had to take.

CHAPTER THREE

JUST AFTER LUNCHTIME, Skylar boarded the crowded bus, hardly about to spend any of her savings by charting a helicopter like the other party guests would. Most of them didn't have to earn their own money. She used the hours to get on top of the work she'd not got to this morning. But as the bus neared her destination, her heart grew heavy. She hadn't been home since her father had passed unexpectedly two years ago. She'd packed up their old little apartment and not looked back. She'd just kept her head down at Helberg, knowing how proud her father had been of her achievements. Loyalty was everything—he'd drilled that into her over and over and she still felt the need to repay that debt. So she wasn't going to let Zane tear her company apart like it was nothing. Her colleagues were her family and they were stressed enough in the face of a difficult retail climate. But she'd seen Zane's stone-cold centre and she had to know his plans for sure.

'Wow.' Danielle greeted her with a wide smile and a huge hug. 'You look amazing.'

Yeah, her make-up, dress and shoes weren't exactly her usual sedate style. She'd had limited options, what with almost every store closed for the holiday. Having to wear white but not wanting to look *bridal* meant she'd had to take the silk dress that skimmed her figure a touch too close, plus had a high split to the side of the long skirt.

'And you're still rocking that high ponytail.' Danielle winked as she handed Skylar a cocktail.

Yeah, long hair tied up was still her thing. It wasn't exactly deliberate. She just never took the time off to get to the hairdressers often and it was easier to keep the length out of her face by either braid or ponytail.

Squaring her shoulders, she sallied forth into the party. She could do this.

Within ten minutes, she knew she'd made a mistake. There were too many people. While she could hold her own in a work meeting, this sort of socialising didn't come naturally. Attending that private school should have helped but in fact had only made her reticence worse. Her father had taught her that trust took a long time to build and was easily destroyed. She had to be careful. Maintaining relationships took a lot of effort, so she had few. Her work was her constant focus, which was why she'd do anything to save it—even engage with the destroyer himself. But as time ticked by, he didn't show and her discomfort increased.

Seeking space, she stepped outside. The lush green lawns leading to the beach were immaculately groomed and she wistfully thought of her father, who'd have been spotting the rare patch that needed work. She walked along the thick hedgerow that formed the side boundary to another palatial holiday home next door. There was a gap along the row and she turned into it, following the path before stopping, surprised to discover a secret garden before her—a rectangular space filled with mature fruit trees, a couple of sun loungers placed in their shade. Completely hidden from view of the houses, the stunning little sanctuary had obviously been here for decades.

She inhaled deep and relaxed properly for the first time in days. Tossing her small bag on the nearest lounger, she strolled beneath the shade of the pretty fruit trees, holding her long ponytail up high so she could feel the slight breeze on her back.

'What are you doing?' a low drawl sounded right behind her.

She spun, dropping her arm. 'What—'

She jerked to a halt, her hair pulling hard as she tried to step back. It took a blink before she realised her ponytail had caught on the low-slung branch above as she'd turned. Now she tried to shake it free with a nonchalant jerk of her head. She failed.

Ridiculous.

He was staring at her wide-eyed. *Him*—breaker of hearts, destroyer of moods, thief of peace. Zane deMarco himself.

'Now look what you…' She trailed off, mortified as she reached up blindly and tried to detangle the long strands caught above her.

Of all the people to startle her into a completely humiliating position… All she could hope now was that he'd not recognise her. The odds had to be in her favour given it had been years since the last time they'd crossed paths, and right now she was out of context, what with her heavy make-up and a slinkier-than-usual dress and please, please, please let him be so sated with so many women they'd all merged into one and he'd never remember the girl he'd once kissed in a cold stairwell early on a Saturday morning…

'You know the cherries aren't anywhere near ripe.' He stood three feet away, taking her in with a sweeping, sardonic gaze that went from her tangled hair to her silver-sandaled feet.

His attention made her very aware of her vulnerability—her raised arms made her dress cling even more to parts of her figure. Parts that all of a sudden tightened with pure chemical awareness. She dropped her hands to her sides with a slap and glared at him.

'What are you doing out here?' he repeated softly. 'Were you trying to find me?'

'Of course not,' she snapped. Even though she was here to do *exactly* that, it was still so arrogant of him to assume. 'I had no idea anyone was out here. I was just—' She broke off as she realised he was still looking her over in that slow, deliberate way, and it felt too *intimate*. Suddenly it didn't matter what she was doing or why she was here; she just needed to escape. ASAP. 'Are you going to help me or just stand there being entertained by my suffering?'

He moved closer. The light stubble on his jaw didn't mask the honed angles beneath and while his mouth was curved in an annoying smirk, his pale blue eyes gleamed with rapier-sharp scrutiny.

Skylar could meet that intense gaze for only so long before she had to lower her lashes. He was wearing black tailored trousers and a white dress shirt, which was unbuttoned at both the collar and sleeves. Indeed, those sleeves were rolled back, revealing strong, sinewy forearms. She gritted her teeth but still her traitorous pulse skipped every other beat as she remembered the strength in his arms. He was a jerk but her stupid body didn't seem to care. It was almost a decade ago, for heaven's sake. It was *not* yesterday.

'You're actually, seriously caught?' he asked sceptically.

'Obviously, or I'd have run away the second you appeared,' she muttered.

'Really?' He looked arrogantly disbelieving.

'Yes, really.'

'And somehow it's all my fault?' he murmured.

Quite. She'd seriously underestimated the impact of seeing him again, and now here she was—*stuck*—but feeling that same insanity she'd felt every time she'd been in his presence. Her tongue was tied, her mind was mince and prickly heat spread across her skin.

Summon anger.

Unfortunately, anger didn't show up. She simply stared into his striking eyes while thoughts of fallen angels and devilish temptations flitted in and out of her scattered brain. Seconds became centuries. Everything slowed as deep inside something fizzed, bubbling higher and higher and hotter and hotter. She had to be ill. Surely. Sudden onset of a strange virus.

'Are you going to help me?' She eventually croaked out another request, because all he seemed to be doing was staring right back at her and standing as still as she was.

'I'm working out the best strategy to extract you from this disaster.'

'I thought you were meant to be a genius.'

His pale blue eyes lit and that was almost the end of her—spontaneous combustion imminent. She closed her eyes. She *couldn't* be feeling this. Nope. Not over Zane. Not again. She was *not* sixteen and full of impossible fantasy now.

She *knew* him—remember? She knew how cold he really was inside. How quickly, how easily he could walk away. He did not care about anything or anyone—

She dragged in a breath but was further intoxicated by the subtle scents of salt and musk and something a touch rougher. Whisky. Every sense ignited. Desperately she stood stock-still, held her breath and kept her eyes screwed shut.

'Skylar?' he murmured huskily. 'You still with me?'

Oh, *hell*. Her eyes flashed open. So did her jaw. Of course her hope that he wouldn't remember her would be futile. He probably had one of those eidetic memories with every minuscule detail of his life stored inside his annoyingly intelligent brain.

'What, did you think I didn't recognise you?' His eyes widened—almost revealing pique. 'Of course I recognised you...'

He raked his gaze down her yet again, taking in the delicate ribbon straps at the base of her neck. The halterneck style meant she was unable to wear a bra beneath it—though to be fair she didn't really need a bra. But as his gaze swept down her, she felt her breasts respond again as if his glance were actually a stroke. Infuriated with herself, she willed her gaze to be more of a slap back. But when he lifted his focus back to her eyes, his smile merely widened from smirk to blindingly gorgeous.

'Just as you recognise me,' he added.

Well duh, of course she did. He was currently wallpapering the internet—one billionaire catch of the day. But okay, yes, it was because she'd spent most of her adult life trying to forget him.

Such things were impossible.

'We lived in the same apartment complex as kids,' he said conversationally as he stepped closer.

She struggled to retain her composure, glad he'd opted for that detail, not the fact they'd once been smashed together, frantically kissing against the wall of said apartment complex. Maybe he'd forgotten that had even happened. She could only hope. 'That's a long time ago now.'

He nodded and reached above her head. 'It doesn't exist any more.'

She took a quick, sharp breath. She'd not been back to their village since her father had passed. She hadn't known the building had been demolished. 'A lot has changed.'

'A lot certainly has,' he agreed with that mocking edge.

He'd been handsome then and he was stunning now. It was severely unfair for one person to get everything—extreme brains and extreme beauty. And she was just like every other woman who came close to him—unable to resist drinking in the sight of his sleek, fit body as he ran his fingers along the length of her hair, trying to smooth it free from the branch. She quelled her shiver but now her pulse thundered. This was way too intimate.

'Your ponytail is very long,' he said. 'Is it all your own?'

'What?' She jerked and her hair tightened again. 'Of course it's mine.'

He laughed beneath his breath. Her mood sharpened. Retaliation was required.

'I've thought you'd manage this more quickly,' she murmured saltily. 'Given you're supposed to be good with your hands.'

He stilled, mere millimetres away from her. Skylar took a second to replay what she'd just said and realised how stupid it was. How incendiary. How easily it would be interpreted as a tragic attempt at flirtation. But before she could backpedal he leaned closer still and resumed his effort to detangle her.

'Oh, I'm very good with my hands,' he drawled softly right near her ear. 'And slow is better, don't you agree?'

No, she did *not* agree. Because the century-length seconds had slowed even more and she wasn't coping.

'Oh, yeah,' he muttered into the thickened silence. 'I should have remembered that you prefer things fast...'

She couldn't reply and he bent to look into her face.

There was that mockery in his eyes, but there was heat too—heat that made that fizzing inside even more intense. If she were normal, she'd laugh this off with some flippant comment. But she wasn't normal. She couldn't think of anything flippant. She couldn't think of anything at all except—

'Just hurry up and finish,' she whispered, unable to believe what both her brain and body wanted.

'Wow,' hc breathed back. 'There's a first.'

She clenched her fists and battled to hold herself back. 'You're not used to your attentions being unwanted?'

His smile of disbelief spread wider. 'But you're the one who asked me to help,' he pointed out. 'I'm being gentlemanly here, rescuing you from the evil clutches of a cherry tree.'

She couldn't laugh. Quicksilver, not blood, flowed in her veins. Handsome in pictures, devastating in the flesh, Zane deMarco embodied sensual vitality, and every breath, every glance, every moment basking in his attention sent Skylar further along the path towards total brainlessness.

His dilating pupils were the only movement he made. 'It really bothers you that I'm this close?'

Dynamite, meet detonator. His mere proximity provided the shock wave to ignite something within her that had long been—well—dead. He wasn't just hard to handle, he was impossible to ignore, and unfathomably that ancient crush just…resurged. Even when she knew what a callous lump of a heart he had, her body didn't care. Her body simply sizzled.

He suddenly moved. She felt loosening at her scalp and his fingers finally ran the full length of her hair and when they hit the end her ponytail fell back to rest against the bared skin of her back.

'There you go—free of me at last. Quick, get away while you can,' he jeered huskily. Bitterness glittered in his eyes. 'There's no one here to rescue you this time. You'd better run inside for safety.'

That was what she'd done almost a decade ago. Run inside and shut the curtains and not peeked out.

But she still couldn't move. She watched that flicker in his eyes and the sardonic curve of his full lips and decided she *wouldn't* give him the satisfaction of running scared. Because when she'd run all those years ago it hadn't been from him.

In truth, right now she was more scared of herself. But she'd come here for information, and while this was hardly the ideal interaction, at least she'd made contact. And suddenly there was an imp within that simply spoke for her.

'Oh, no.' She flicked her hand through her hair and the swish of her ponytail basically hit him in the nose. 'I'm not going anywhere. That would be far too easy for you.'

'You're here to make things hard for me?' Zane jammed his tingling hands into his pockets. He was hard already in a shockingly instant reaction to this unexpected encounter. He hadn't been going to bother with Danielle's party. He'd flown up later than intended and been late to cut across the garden, and as he had he'd glimpsed a nymph in the orchard and investigated only to find—

Skylar Bennet.

Hers was a face from the past that he preferred to keep well behind him, and he'd certainly not expected to see her here and looking like this. Not all glossy hair, glossy lips, glossy dress…not the perfectly polite, dutifully docile, completely irritating swot he knew Skylar was.

So he could do nothing but stare. The white silk clung to

her slender curves, and a high split in the skirt teased flashes of skin while a thin ribbon at her neck secured the dress. He wanted to tug on the ends and watch it all slip from her silky-looking skin. He wanted to see the secrets beneath. He wanted to free her hair and feel it trail and tease his skin—and all but whip him in the face again.

Of course, the truth was he'd wanted all that since he'd been eighteen and guiltily watching her comb her hair at her window across the courtyard and up one floor from his. And he'd not been allowed then, had he? Her father had informed him he'd never, ever be good enough for her. And yeah, he certainly wouldn't be good enough in that man's eyes now.

Only now here she was in front of him again. He'd not expected her to be so tartly defensive. She'd verbally lashed him like a little wild creature caught in the bushes. Except she wasn't so little. Not in the good places. He'd reacted. So had she. Sexual tension had taken command of them both.

'Maybe I am,' she huskily countered.

Sexual tension was *definitely* still in charge. His muscles bunched as he watched the tilt of her chin and the antagonism build in her eyes.

She'd grown up in that third-floor apartment opposite his. A pretty, petite brunette with the biggest brown eyes he'd ever seen. He'd struggled with his own issues back then—all that time it had taken to heal after the accident, the risky moves he'd been making with his online trading platform, desperately trying to make money to get out of there, but she'd been a constant in the background. A fellow battler on the block. Another only child of a solo parent. She'd been better than him though—she'd been *good*. She'd been so intensely focused on her studies she'd won one of Reed Helberg's prestigious scholarships.

And she'd gone.

But the shy, pretty girl he'd occasionally seen had come back from her fancy new boarding school for the holidays and somehow been completely different. She'd sat on her balcony in the shade and studied all damned day, only moving to make her father meals or fetch his drinks when he returned from work. The only time Zane saw her leave that apartment was to go for a morning run. A new routine. He'd seen her smile and heard her soft laughter as she'd chatted to her father. They'd seemed close. And Zane had been so smitten, he'd loitered in the courtyard at her run time like a lovesick fool. And one morning, for just a few stolen moments, he'd tasted her.

Before she'd turned her back and betrayed him.

He'd not seen her again before she'd gone back to school and then he'd left town. They'd been at that stupid dinner at his old school where he'd been guest speaker a couple years later. He'd been flattered by the invite and had said yes. He'd not made that mistake again. Reed Helberg had been there and Skylar had been so perfect and polite. She'd not even looked at Zane; everything had been about Reed. He'd been infuriated—because of her desperation to please, right? She'd won what he'd been denied but his irritation hadn't been because of that. He'd hated that demure demeanour—that her docility was so underpinned by anxiety. Wide-eyed and terrified by the supposed importance of the old man who'd dominated the dinner conversation. Those stupid scholarships might supposedly be life-changing, but in Zane's opinion, the price paid by the winner was too high. It was all so wretchedly *controlling*.

But now Skylar Bennet was entirely grown-up and all alone and apparently here to make things hard for him. Well, she'd succeeded.

'So you did come here to see me,' he said, feeling visceral pleasure at the thought.

She stared at him—basically breathing fire. His recklessness surged as he watched the enmity battle the interest burgeoning in her deep brown eyes. He wanted to turn that gleam into sleepy satisfaction. He lost track of everything else. Where he was going. Why. What he was meant to do and not do...none of it mattered. Because he could see only her and right now he wanted nothing but her.

That old desire slammed back into him. He'd wanted her so much back then—with all the ardour of inexperience and youth. She'd been tantalisingly close, yet so out of bounds. Maybe that was why it was back so fiercely now. She'd been his first crush—wholly forbidden fruit.

'You don't usually come to this party.' His throat tightened. He'd liked touching her hair. It was long, silky, fragrant, and he battled the sharp urge to release it from that tight band now.

She stiffened as he stepped closer.

He suppressed his smile with difficulty. It was harder to suppress everything around her. 'You still don't party much? Ever the hard worker, Skylar?'

She was quiet and dutiful while he wasn't. Maybe it was the simple, strong magnetism of polar opposites, because she couldn't seem to take a step from him. Nor could he from her. The defiance in her brown eyes deepened.

'You've not bothered to pay attention to the dress code, I see,' she said coolly. 'At least I've made the effort to do as asked.'

'Of course you have,' he murmured insolently. 'I bet you always do as you're asked...' He couldn't resist stepping closer. 'Like a good girl.'

Her eyes narrowed.

'You always were so *obedient*,' he growled, scrambling to stop the racing thoughts rising from his own damned words. '*Such* a pleaser.'

God, he wanted her to please him. And he wouldn't just please her back. He'd destroy her.

Because all those years ago she'd gone up in flames in his arms. He'd almost lost his footing she'd been so passionate—she'd wanted him every bit as much as he'd wanted her. But she'd not defended him when her father had thought the worst of him. How she'd silently abandoned him as they'd faced her father's wrath and rejection. He couldn't forgive her for that. But nor could he forget that *she'd* been the one rubbing against him in the most arousing of ways. *She'd* been the one moaning. *She'd* been the one shaking. It had taken every ounce of his utterly limited experience back then to try to slow them down. Because it had been a conflagration. And he was so close to every brain cell burning up again now.

'While you're a taker,' she replied tartly.

He smiled wolfishly, enjoying her attack. 'You think?' Spreading his hands wide in innocence, he shot her a look. 'But tell me, how can I wear all white when I'm prone to getting a little dirty?'

Her eyes widened and twin spots of colour deepened in her cheeks. He was unrepentant. She was the one who'd started this—even if that earlier innuendo had been unintentional. But they had chemistry and it wouldn't be curbed. Zane was all for fireworks now they were adults. Fireworks were fun.

'Or maybe it's just that you think the rules don't apply to you,' she said.

'Rules?' He faux shivered, as if she'd raised a horrifying spectre.

His little nemesis rolled her eyes. 'You won't ever do what others ask of you,' she said with soft precision. 'You're too arrogant.'

Every rule jumped out the window.

'You think?' he breathed. 'Why don't you find out for yourself?' He was a millimetre from her pretty face, willing her to take what he was really offering. 'Go on, Skylar. Ask me anything. *I dare you.*'

CHAPTER FOUR

OH, SHE'D DARE...

But she didn't. Old habits were hard to break. She just had to back away slowly. Take the exit via the beach.

'You can't go yet,' he said softly.

'Why not?' She glared at him.

'You really have to ask?'

A moment of searing tension strung her out before she shook her head sceptically. While she was thinking wildly inappropriate things about him, he was merely toying with her. That was what he did. 'Oh, please.'

He stood very, very still—his hands still in his pockets—as a faint flush coloured his sculpted cheeks. He was insanely handsome but he didn't mean anything in this moment. He could turn his charm off and on like a switch.

'I didn't get a thank-you,' he said eventually.

'You'd be satisfied with a mere thank-you?'

'Yeah, no. You're right. Actions do speak louder than words.'

What kind of *actions* was he thinking of? She glared at him. 'You want a ticker tape parade for acting like a decent human?'

'Maybe you might offer to get me a drink,' he said.

'You're thirsty?'

His smile appeared. 'You have to agree it's very hot out here.'

She shot him another withering look, but she was the one withering inside. *Run.*

'Still no thank-you?' he said after a moment. 'When I rescued you so gallantly?' He tut-tutted. 'You do intrigue me, Skylar.'

'Am I supposed to be pleased about that?' She folded her arms across her chest and wished for inches.

'You're saying you're not?' His grin widened. 'But maybe you're not *quite* as polite as you've always appeared.' His eyes gleamed. 'Maybe you sometimes like to get dirty too. In fact, I'm sure you do.'

Her breath stalled. She couldn't answer that.

'Thanks or not, I'm glad I was here to help,' he added. 'Your hair is stunning. It would be devastating if it were damaged.'

Devastating? She felt an absurd pleasure that he liked her hair. And it *was* absurd, because she also knew this was just another of his lines. 'You really can't stop yourself, can you?'

'Stop myself from what?'

'Flirting.'

The corner of his lush mouth curved. 'You think this is me flirting?'

Die. Again. Just die.

He walked so close that she had to step back. And she kept stepping until the backs of her legs hit the sun lounger. That's when she was forced to stop. But he didn't stop. Not until he was less than a breath apart from her.

'You definitely weren't at this party last year,' he said softly. 'You're *never* at these sorts of parties.'

She tossed her head. 'What makes you so sure?'

His voice dropped. 'I'd have noticed.'

Her temperature rose. She dragged in a searing breath. 'No you wouldn't—'

He reached out and gently flicked a wisp of hair from her face. His hand landed on her waist when he lowered it.

'What are you doing?' she stammered.

He smiled indulgently, his blue gaze intent on her. 'This is me flirting.'

'This isn't flirting, this is just you…crowding me.'

'Too close?' he breathed. 'Shall I step back?'

His ice blue gaze locked on her for a long moment. She was toe-curlingly hot and she couldn't possibly be wanting what she was thinking. She was supposed to be here to ask him about Helberg—only suddenly she didn't want to think about any of that. Suddenly she didn't want to think about anything at all.

'I don't think you want me to step back,' he whispered. 'I think you want me to stay right where I am.' He cocked his head. 'I think you want other things as well. So let me dare you again, Skylar…*ask me.*'

She swallowed. She should shut this down right now but she simply couldn't, such was his potency. 'You get what *you* want far too easily,' she muttered feebly.

'And?' He slid that hand around her waist, his broad palm spread wide and flat on her back. The heat and strength of him through the thin silk was both arousing and oddly *reassuring…*

She'd been here before and once more she couldn't move. He was the biggest tease and she was falling for it—letting him all over again—because yeah, just like that, she was a *yes.*

'Do you want me to walk away?' he challenged her huskily.

But he was serious. She realised that with one word from

her, he would leave. He would not look back. Once again, it would be like this moment had never ever happened.

And suddenly she couldn't speak. She couldn't lie and send him from her. Because this was every unfinished fantasy she'd ever had. And she was furious about it.

At university *years* later, she'd tried to find this fire with someone else. She'd let another guy kiss her. It had left her cold. She'd kissed a different one. Same deal. She'd wondered if maybe her father catching her had caused some shame that she needed time to get over. It had been a relief to think that. A relief not to try anything more with anyone else ever.

But now it destroyed something in her to realise that it wasn't that at all. Because she still responded to *Zane*. Right here. Right now. She was aroused. And maybe that wouldn't happen with anyone else while *he* was still in her system. How hideous that he was the only man who she responded to in this insanely intense way. That had to be fixed.

In this second, what happened with Helberg Holdings was irrelevant. There was no one around to interrupt them. No one to tell her *not* to dare...

She needed to get over this stupid hang-up. And maybe that was by having what she wanted from him. As galling as it might be to add herself to his list of conquests, maybe she'd be free of her fixation on him at last.

'Stop teasing me,' she snapped jerkily. 'So far you're all talk.'

Surprise flashed in his eyes, followed swiftly by a flare of satisfaction. Both were engulfed in the blue-black heat of engorged pupils. He didn't wait for her to change her mind. His hand at her back firmed, pushing her close so they were suddenly belly to belly and he'd proven he wasn't all tease.

He promised very real passion. She gasped as he anchored her to his hard body and as she did, he lowered his head.

'Will you taste of raspberry candy this time, Skylar?'

She shook her head. She'd not had raspberry candy in years—it was too associated with him. 'I prefer lemon.'

'Right,' he muttered. 'Apparently you've become a little acid drop.'

Taking total advantage of her parted lips, he kissed her—deeply, intimately, endlessly.

Boom. Combustion of epic proportions.

She threw her arms around his neck and held on, tangling her tongue with his, pressing her pelvis closer to his. Power surged and she was out of control all over again. But he didn't press his forehead on hers and croon her name beneath his breath this time. His hands didn't tremble as he ran them down her arms. He just demanded her response—and devoured her.

But one thing remained the same. She felt wanted. Absolutely, utterly *wanted*. And she wanted him right back. Wholly sexually, right?

Wholly unbearably.

He pressed her closer still, grinding her body against his. She had no idea how long they were plastered to each other, frantically kissing. It was an inferno in seconds, every kiss better and better until her whole body quaked with desperation.

Of *course* he was a complete philanderer. Good for all those women who'd enjoyed this experience. She wasn't going to deny herself just to teach him a lesson he was never going to care about. She was going to take what she wanted. And that was this. Him. Now. Nothing else mattered. The kissing went on—hotter, more erotic, more hungry. She wriggled, helplessly aching and restless. Until he suddenly tore his lips from hers.

'Don't you want to know what I want?' he growled breathlessly.

This *should* be a two-way thing, but now he'd found that split in her skirt and his fingers were sliding up her leg—skin on skin—and she was so overwhelmed, so afraid of him stopping, she didn't want to admit how much this suddenly mattered.

'Do you think I care?' she asked.

He laughed, and the vibrations resonated deep in her belly and turned her on even more.

'Oh, I know you care,' he teased, and kissed her again as if it were all reward. 'Bleeding-heart little pleaser like you can't help *caring*.'

She leaned back, letting her pelvis grind harder against his even as she glared at him. 'For the record, I do *not* care about *you*.'

'You think you dislike me as much as I dislike you?' But his hand hit her panties as he taunted her. His fingers twisted. With total strength, he tore the lace so he could target her...*there*. 'You annoy the hell out of me, Skylar,' he growled.

But his fingers teased, skilful, utterly intimate little strokes that matched the magic he worked with his mouth as he pressed lush kisses across her face and neck. She began to tremble, and that's when he leaned closer still. His whisper was hot, his lips brushing just beneath her earlobe on that ultra-sensitive skin of her neck. 'So I want to see you crumble.'

His blistering focus—his irritation with his own attention on her—pulsated within her. Deeply. Their antagonism was real and couldn't be resolved. The fact was she didn't like him. And he didn't like her.

'Then make me,' she dared.

'It'll be my damned pleasure.' He lowered his lips that last millimetre back to her skin and licked his way down to the neckline. 'There's no one around to stop me now. And I know you won't.'

Skylar shivered, breathless and hot as he kissed beyond and below—all the way to her breast. He didn't care about the silk. He sucked on her taut nipple straight through it as his fingers twisted and slid right inside her.

She came. Hard. Bucking her hips, she writhed on his hand and arched her back so he could mouth more of her breast. She was greedy. Fortunately, so was he.

His arm was an iron rod at her back, but even so, she barely remained upright. He lowered her with a rough laugh, straight onto the sun lounger behind her, and followed her.

'Oh, you do like it fast,' he muttered. 'Even faster than I'd expected.'

Bliss pulsated in rivulets down her body but that cord of sexual tension wasn't yet severed. 'You're a supercilious jerk, you know that?'

He nuzzled his way back up her neck. 'And you're a sanctimonious swot.' He reared up and looked into her eyes. 'So what? We're still going to have sex.'

And there it was. She stilled, staring up into his eyes and seeing the intent. The invitation. The opportunity of a lifetime. His pelvis dug into hers so she had no doubts about whether he really wanted this. But she registered his hesitation—his query. If she were her normal self, she'd say *no* instantly. But she wasn't just tempted nor just curious—she was so unbearably turned on there wasn't time to think about it. 'Of course we are,' she snapped. 'Just hurry the hell up!'

His laugh this time was low and exultant and he dropped back down to kiss her—pure reward, pure tease.

'Not *so* fast, this time.' He reached up and freed her ponytail from the tight elastic. He ran his hand through the thick length of her hair in an intensely intimate caress. It felt like he was worshipping her. But surely not—it was just that he was pure hedonist. A sensualist who enjoyed all touch. And right now, so did she.

'You've changed, Skylar Bennet,' he muttered as he pulled at the ribbons of her halter neck.

For the first time nerves fluttered. 'Not so much, I'm as f-flat-chested as ever...'

He glanced up, wide-eyed but laughing.

'Wouldn't want you to be disappointed.' She flushed with annoyance at the self-conscious wail that had escaped her before she could stop it. But the man had had a million lovers.

'Not gonna be,' he said. 'Vexed by your mouth, maybe. Never, ever disappointed by your body.'

The silk finally slid, exposing her breasts. He just stared and she felt him take in a deep breath and harden even more against her. To her total mortification, as he pressed closer, she just came all over again. Shivers of sensual bliss shook her.

'Hell, Skylar...' he hissed. 'Should've known you'd be exceptional in every thing you do.'

She was too far gone in her bliss bubble to be able to answer. But he thought she was exceptional?

'Don't think you're done,' he whispered. 'Not done yet. Not without me.'

He rose to his knees and reached into his pocket. He

had protection with him. Other than a quick feeling of relief, she didn't give that fact a second thought. There was
no time for thinking. Only feeling. Moving. Teasing with
a kind of anger that came from someplace she didn't really understand. But she suddenly wanted him to feel this
as urgently as she.

He didn't bother stripping entirely. He just unfastened
his trousers and yanked his boxers down enough to roll on
the condom. There was no time to get her completely free
of her dress, so he just slid her skirt up. Her panties were
little more than shredded lace on a waistband and were no
obstacle at all.

He paused for a moment, his hand flat on her lower belly,
and shook his head as he stared at her. 'Skylar—'

She growled and shifted restlessly beneath him and with
a groan he just kissed her. A second later, his full weight
was on her and it was everything. He grabbed her thigh
with his big hand and lifted her leg over his hip to make
more space for him. And then he was there. She shuddered
as he breached her virgin body with his.

'Hell,' he choked. 'I'm gonna—' He broke off with a
groan and gritted his teeth. Lodged hard and deep inside
her, his muscles bunched beneath her hands. 'I want—' He
broke off again. 'You—'

He was so breathless, panting hard as if he faced a battle
he knew he couldn't win. His struggle for control snapped
hers. Heat surged, chasing away the tiny pinch of pain that
had halted her breath when he'd first pushed inside her. She
grabbed his hips, suddenly hungry for more, and writhed
beneath him. She desperately needed him to move.

'Damn it, Skylar!' he roared. 'You're not making me—'

He pulled right out of her and she moaned at the loss in

agonised frustration. But he half laughed before drawing in several steadying breaths.

'*My* pace, princess,' he finally said as he held her fast and slowly reclaimed his place deep inside her.

There was no pinch this time—only a sensation so intense that she could scarcely sigh as he leisurely rolled his hips and slid fractionally deeper with each powerful thrust.

'That's it,' he muttered. 'Stay with me now.'

Oh, she was with him—imprisoned in his embrace, impaled on his shaft—it was the best torture ever. With slow decadence he moved within her. The pull and drag of the friction between them was the most exquisite sensation of her life. She'd always felt so awkward around others that any kind of physical intimacy had felt impossible. But this with him was simply *effortless*. And so exciting. Which was also *so* annoying.

'I hate you,' she muttered breathlessly even as she clutched him closer, instinctively arching her hips to meet his over and over in this dance.

Humour-laced passion glittered in his eyes. 'Want me to hurry up and finish?'

She helplessly mumbled a meaningless denial. She sighed and stirred, matching his moves with the answering arch of her hips. It was fun. And good. And now she really did want it faster. And harder. And more all over again.

His choked laughter was followed by an explicit curse. She slid her hand into his hair and kissed him. His hands tightened and his movements roughened, his possession deepened even more. She broke free and gasped and as her orgasm rushed upon her, she realised he too had finally lost it.

There was no kissing in those last frantic moments. Only his harsh whispers—his intentions of dirty and deep possession savagely and repeatedly sworn. It was so hot that she shook in ecstasy all over again.

The last thing she heard was her name—uttered as if it were a curse as he came hard inside her.

CHAPTER FIVE

'Skylar?'

Lost in a sensorial haze, Skylar kept her eyes closed as she breathed in the balmy air, savouring the sultry scents of salt and heat and musk. She'd just had sex. For the first time. Outside in a garden, mere metres from a gathering of some of the most rich and powerful people in the country. Sex with Zane deMarco in fact. The guy she loved to hate. And as he was still holding her, still inside her, there was no escaping that reality.

But she didn't *want* to escape. She wanted to stay right here, for good. Because even though he was heavy, she was somehow floating in a rapturous state unlike anything she'd known. She felt weightless and lax and utterly relaxed and she didn't want it to end.

'Skylar?'

There was a tone in his voice that she didn't recognise. Opening her eyes, she saw he'd eased up onto his elbows and was staring down at her. The haze she'd been enmeshed in slowly dispersed and in her reluctant return to reality, a top-to-toe tremble racked her body.

'You're cold,' he said gruffly.

That hadn't been a shiver but an aftershock of epic proportions. Hardly surprising given the intense experience her nervous system had just endured. She'd gone from first intimate touch to triple orgasm in minutes. Searing, sweet minutes that she ached to savour. She still didn't want it to be over.

But too carefully, too swiftly, he levered himself off her and stood. He wasn't smiling any more. There wasn't any of that smooth tease she'd expect—in fact, he looked as awkward as she felt as he turned away to haul up his trousers.

Did he regret this already? Doubts flurried in. She'd been inexperienced. Maybe it hadn't been all that for him.

Her heart was still thundering as she sat up and awkwardly swung her legs to stand. She'd lost some coordination and the crumpled silk dress that had been bunched around her waist now slid to the grass as she half stumbled to her feet.

Great. Now she was fully naked—aside from the high-heeled sandals that made little difference in getting her anywhere near his height. Zane bent and retrieved her dress from the ground before she could think to beat him to it.

He frowned and gave it a shake and frowned. 'I don't know how we got grass stains...' He lifted it higher so he could see it more clearly in the fading light. 'Not grass. Blood.'

Horrified, Skylar bent her head, letting her hair hide her face and half her super-sensitive body while she took a deep breath.

But Zane spoke again before she could. 'You have your period? Do you need me to get you some—'

'I'm fine. It's fine. I'm not— I don't need anything.' Except a magic wand with which to vanish. Instantly. Only they didn't exist so she was going to have to bone up and deal with the reality. Bluntly. Honestly. Matter-of-factly.

The man was so comfortable around women that he thought nothing of discussing something she found deeply personal.

'But—'

'I was a virgin,' she blurted. 'Don't worry about it.'

'A what?' He stared at her and crushed the dress in his hands. 'A *what*?'

She licked her lips nervously. 'First-timer. Let's forget it.'

'You were a virgin?' He snatched a breath and repeated it again. 'A *virgin*?'

Her annoyance returned. Which was good. 'Say it again, you might understand it next time.'

'A… You…' He drew in another breath. 'I've never taken anyone's virginity.' He stared down at her grimly.

'I guess there's a first for everything.' She winced.

He dropped her dress back to the ground and ran his hand through his hair a couple times. 'You shouldn't have— what were you *thinking*?'

'I wasn't. Obviously. Same as you.' She cleared her throat. 'If it's such an issue, just forget it ever happened.'

'Forget?' He threw her an astounded look, which morphed to furious in a nanosecond.

She wasn't sure why he was suddenly so angry. But as he stalked towards her, Skylar held her stance, crossing her arms but wincing inwardly at her nudity. He stopped three feet away, shrugged off his shirt and held it out to her.

'Put it on,' he ordered after a moment.

At her continued hesitation he grew more grim. 'Do you really want to walk back through that party with all those people in a crumpled, stained dress and have absolutely everyone know exactly what we've been doing?'

She snatched the shirt from his hand and slid her arms into the sleeves. It was still warm from his body and it hung to her mid-thigh and it smelt of him and she shivered again. His jaw sharpened but he said nothing more.

She bent and picked up her bag. 'I'll—'

'Come with me.' His grip on her wrist was firm.

'Come with you *where*?' she demanded curtly. 'I'm not going through that party like this *either*.'

'Come with me to a "where" with privacy. A shower. Food. *Drink*.' He muttered beneath his breath. 'And more damned clothes.'

He led her through that garden to a different gap in the hedge, then walked up the path to the palatial house next door.

'We can't just walk into someone else's house,' she whispered, scandalised as he boldly led her up the path.

'We're not. We've been on my property this whole time.'

'What?'

'That orchard is on my side of the boundary and this is my house.'

She yanked her arm free of his hold and whirled to stare at him. 'Since when is this *your* house?'

He simply sidestepped around her. 'Since a month ago.'

Once more she wished for the magic vanishing wand.

He opened the door with a singular touch to a small tech pad. The house was stunning. Comfortable and homely. The furnishings cosy and somehow not what she would've expected from Zane deMarco, ruthless corporate raider. But Zane deMarco, as a teen, housebound while recovering from injury, might have wanted something exactly this comfortable.

He was watching her sardonically. 'I bought it furnished.'

Right. Of course. This was someone else's sense of happiness and intimacy. He was corporate raider Zane now, through and through.

'Come on.'

He didn't seem able to look at her for long. Her self-consciousness grew. She probably looked a sight. Loose, her hair hung to just below her buttocks and was no doubt tangled. His white shirt was smudged and creased and also hung to below her buttocks. But it was only because of her lack of clothes that she was still here, grudgingly going along with his suggestions.

He led the way down the hallway and up the stairs and she followed him mutely. He walked her into a gorgeous bedroom.

'You need to have a shower,' he grated. 'Get dressed. Warm.'

Huh, she was boiling already.

'Wait here a moment.'

It was less than a minute before he was back and handing her a bundle of sweats. She took them from him but he paused. He stared at her for a long, long moment. The heat that had overwhelmed her so instantly earlier now resurged. For a split second she hoped he was about to tumble her to the bed they were standing beside.

'I'll take the other shower,' he said tightly. 'Don't even think about vanishing on me.'

He turned his back on her and stomped out so quickly her head spun.

It was one of those showers that had nozzles pointing in every direction that gave her a whole-body massage effect. It was the second-most sensual experience of her life. She lost track of time again before coming back to herself and turning the water off hurriedly.

She needed to get out of here. She'd get changed. Get

back to her little motel. Get space to get her head around everything. Because she'd royally screwed up. Yet she couldn't quite regret it.

She plaited her hair to keep it out of the way and pulled on the sweatpants. They were so big she had to roll the waist over several times. They were definitely his. And definitely turning her on. Too hot to bother with the sweatshirt he'd put on the pile, she slid on the white T-shirt. It hung like a dress so she knotted the hem, but it made little difference. He'd swamped her in his clothes—hiding her few curves. She couldn't look less sexy and yet her sensual awareness of him couldn't be higher.

She'd had sex with Zane deMarco. Fantastic. Unforgettable. Fiery sex. And all she could think was that she wanted more. Right now in fact. But he clearly didn't because he hadn't been able to get away from her fast enough. Which was mortifying. Wasn't he supposed to be some insatiable playboy?

That's when she finally remembered just who and what he was. Mr One-Date Wonder. The man took what he wanted and moved on and she was such a fool for forgetting for so long tonight.

Red alert, red alert, red alert.

Zane paced in the kitchen. What the *hell* had just happened? And *how* had that just happened? Yeah, he liked sex and honestly got it easy enough, but that was the fastest he'd gone from saying hi to being horizontal. It had been the merest of minutes. And with Skylar Bennet? Petite, perfect student Skylar?

The one he'd wanted long ago and not been allowed. The one who'd said nothing as her father had torn shreds off him—rejecting him as so many others bloody had. Even when he'd just made his first million.

So tonight, when he'd seen her looking at him with those judging eyes, it had all come flooding back and something had snapped. He'd wanted to best her. He'd wanted to win. And he had. In fact he'd just won her *virginity* beneath his damned cherry tree!

And how the hell had *she* still been a virgin? Because honestly, thinking back on that encounter when they were teens, he'd figured she was about the only woman he'd ever met who might have a sex drive to match his...she'd gone up in flames *so* damned quick. But apparently, she'd never gone all the way? What the *hell*? How could he have been so wrong? Had she been saving it for someone? But that didn't make sense when she'd just gone headlong into he-donism with him in seconds. And why hadn't she said any-thing—warned him? Because that hadn't been the gentle initiation he'd have given her had he known. That had been fast and physical and he was *furious* with her for taking that risk with him. He did not want to think that he might have hurt her.

But the fact was he hadn't even had the restraint or pa-tience to bring her the extra few paces into his house and to privacy and clean sheets on an actual bed and with a whole night ahead of them. There'd been nothing but des-perate urgency on a damned narrow sun lounger. He'd had to have her then and there and she'd been five steps ahead of him the whole way...

It had been his hottest moment in months, years— ever—and he wanted it again. Now. The second he'd got her inside his house he'd got hard all over again. He'd had to gruffly hustle her into the guest wing and go take an ice-cold shower. It hadn't worked. He still wanted her. He would give almost anything to linger over her in his big bed right now.

Except she didn't like him. And he didn't like her. And this had been one *massive* mistake.

He stopped pacing and leaned against the counter, staring out at the ocean though it was barely visible now under the night sky. But all he saw was her heart-shaped face and deep brown eyes. Not to mention those plump lips that could go full pout—the sort you could just sink into. And then there was the dimple. It didn't show with a polite smile, nor a restrained smile. But it did with a satisfied post-orgasmic smile. His body went hard as a rock all over again. He reckoned the dimple would show with laughter too. Part of him really wanted to test that theory. But he clenched his fists and summoned restraint. There couldn't be any of that now.

Because he'd finally remembered all the stupid plans he'd made today and this was the *worst* timing imaginable. He wasn't supposed to be fooling around at all let alone with someone horrifyingly innocent. Someone who he didn't even *like*…

But the second he'd seen her in that perfect white silk number he'd forgotten everything. Including that bloody bet.

He'd screwed up. Royally.

Skylar cautiously ventured through the immaculate house that screamed sultry summer energy. It was the perfect place to laze at the beach and indulge in long sensual nights. A heavenly holiday destination, and it honestly just made her angry with him all over again, for buying something so damned perfect that he probably was going to sell in mere months.

She paused on the threshold of the kitchen. He was leaning on the counter, looking out the window, his arms stretched wide in an echo of that night all those years ago when she'd seen him on his balcony. He looked as lonely. But he must've caught sight of her movement because he suddenly turned and his expression smoothed as he walked towards her.

'Are you okay?' he asked with soft intensity.

An unfamiliar emotion clogged her throat.

He walked closer still—until he could take her face in his firm hands so she couldn't look away from him. Couldn't avoid answering him.

'Are. You. Okay?' His pale blue eyes glittered with fire.

For another second she was unable to utter a thing. She swallowed—hard—as she realised the source of his concern. He didn't want to have hurt her. 'Yes, I'm okay.'

In fact she was far better than okay. And she was melting because he was so close and she wanted his mouth on hers again. She wanted *everything* all over again and his concern only made her attraction to him stronger. But he released her and stepped back.

Desolate, she watched him walk away. She didn't want this to be over. Yeah, she was *that* tragic. But he'd moved on while she'd lost sight of everything—of why she'd even come here tonight and what it was she *truly* wanted. Suddenly she was mad with herself for losing her aptitude, her capability. She was no less than he—she didn't need to be *cosseted*.

'Are you?' she called after him sharply.

He paused and glanced back. 'What?'

She walked over to where he stood frozen in the centre of the kitchen. 'Are *you* okay?'

His eyes widened. 'Of course.'

He looked shocked she'd asked.

'Because I didn't mean to give you a fright,' she added calmly. 'And I wanted what happened between us.'

'Right. You know I had worked that one out...' He frowned at her. 'But what I'm not sure about is why you really came to that party in the first place.'

It was her turn to freeze. It all came back—Helberg. Her colleagues, their future. Indeed, her career—the one she'd worked so hard for. The company she desperately wanted to be saved was teetering on the brink of destruction and the man wielding the sword was now standing right in front of her.

'I can't stay the night here.' She glanced away from him.

'I've not asked you to.'

'I'll call a car.'

'The likelihood of you getting any kind of taxi tonight is nil and you know it. I'll take you anywhere you want once we've talked.'

'There's nothing to talk about.'

'Sure there is.' He watched her closely. 'What did you *really* want from me tonight, Skylar?'

Her heart stopped, then pounded faster than ever. This was not how it was supposed to go at all. She'd meant to find out all she could about his plans for Helberg—not find out all about his performance in bed.

And he knew, somehow, that there was more to her appearance tonight. So she might as well just ask him now. Straight-out. She had literally nothing left to lose. 'I wanted to find out your plans for Helberg.'

He stilled. 'What?'

She'd surprised him. 'I know you're interested,' she said firmly.

'Indeed I am,' he answered too smoothly. 'Very much.'

'In *Helberg*,' she said primly, because he was prevaricating now and she wasn't falling for his false charm. 'I don't know what you're planning with those guys but I know it won't be good. Not for the company, its customers or its employees.'

He stepped closer. 'What guys?'

'I saw you this morning. In Manhattan. At that health club.'

He was visibly taken aback. 'You saw me with Cade and Adam?' His jaw tightened. 'Were you spying on me?'

'Of course not.' She was offended. 'I was getting a coffee on my way to work. The cafe isn't far from the office.'

'The *Helberg* office? Don't tell me you're *still* involved with them?' He gaped at her. 'Do they actually pay you now or are you still one of their interns?'

'Of course they pay me now,' she said stiffly, outraged.

'Well, I hope they it's a lot given you were headed there first thing on a Saturday.'

'There's a lot to be done.'

'Certainly is.' He frowned at her. 'Have you ever worked anywhere else?'

She glared at him, not seeing the relevance.

'Loyalty at the cost of your own career?' He shook his head dolefully. 'You really are far too much of a pleaser.'

'So what are your plans?' she asked determinedly. 'I don't think you three were there talking about that article in *Blush*.'

'You've seen *that*?' He was taken aback all over again.

'Hard to miss if you have a phone,' she said.

He leaned back against the bench and folded his arms, watching her acutely. 'Why don't you think we were talking about that?'

'Because you don't care what anyone says or does or thinks about you.'

There was a moment of total silence. A moment in which the world seemed to shrink as he stared right into her soul with those ice blue eyes.

'You think you know me, Skylar?' he asked softly.

'You're saying you do give a damn?' she countered.

He stared at her a second longer than released a pent-up breath. 'I like being my own person. It's liberating. It enables me to make the decisions I want to make. I'm not held back by obligations to others. Unlike you.'

'You think I've been held back?'

'Absolutely.'

'Caring—giving a damn about others and what they may or may not think has never held me back. And fulfilling a duty—repaying a debt—is important.'

'It's stifling,' he dismissed her.

She stepped up to him, toe-to-toe, in her bare feet. 'Helberg shouldn't be ripped apart by a bunch of sharks.'

'A management buy-out isn't going to happen,' he said bluntly. 'Is that what you're hoping for?'

It was exactly what she would have hoped for once, but the current management had proven themselves incompetent and it wasn't going to happen. She needed a better buyer.

'You're right, of course,' Zane suddenly said. 'We're all interested in acquiring Helberg. Which is why you came to this party. Why you sought me out tonight. Are you *that* concerned about your job that you offered yourself as a virgin sacrifice?' His smile wasn't kind. 'Should have negotiated terms first, darling.'

'I was no sacrifice and I didn't tangle myself in that tree deliberately.'

'So what was your original plan in coming here tonight?'

She didn't know. She was an idiot. She'd never really had the confidence nor skill to pull this off. It had been the most ill-conceived plan ever. Employment contracts she could do, but taking on Zane deMarco?

He seemed to take a little pity on her. 'I'm not working with Cade or Adam on this,' he said. 'We each want it for our own reasons. Fortunately we've worked out a way to settle which one of us is going to get it.'

'Really?' She was sceptical. 'You're such arrogant control freaks I'm astounded that you've found a way to do that.'

The smile that slowly creased his face was devilish. 'Well, we billionaires tend to nail creativity.'

'Oh?' She wasn't going to inappropriate places in her head again.

'Yeah.' He watched her closely. 'We've made it the prize of a bet.'

'A *bet*?' She gaped. 'What are the terms?'

CHAPTER SIX

Zane drew a sharp breath and brazened it out. 'We did actually discuss that article this morning. The guys don't like the attention it's bringing to business so we've made a bet to date only one woman over summer.'

'And that's, what—a challenge for you?' she asked caustically.

Amusement rippled within him. He liked sparring with this grown-up, salty Skylar. 'Very, as it so happens.'

A storm gathered in her eyes. 'You're seriously deciding about the fate of a company and all its employees by betting about your *sex lives*?'

'*Dating* lives,' he corrected her facetiously.

And actually it was a *disaster*, because he wasn't going to be able to go anywhere without being photographed alongside someone. He needed a force field around him so no unintentional contact could be misinterpreted.

'No way was this Adam Courtney's idea,' Skylar analysed quickly.

'He only agreed because he thinks he can easily win,' Zane conceded with a grin.

'And *Cade* thinks he can beat you.' Skylar studied him. 'Only a bunch of jerks could sort out a business decision based on their sex lives.'

He felt heat rise even though he was wearing only a thin T-shirt and shorts. 'No one should be writing any stupid articles about our sex lives. We're entitled to privacy as much as anyone else. There's nothing wrong with enjoying the company of other adults and we shouldn't have to moderate our behaviour because of some judgmental hack journalist.'

'Yet you've created a bet requiring you to do exactly that,' she pointed out.

He gritted his teeth. 'It was a vehicle to settle the dispute.'

'It was a whim.' She watched him. 'It was *you* who suggested it, wasn't it. The one *they* think is least likely to succeed.'

Yeah, that too.

'You really enjoy acting on the spur of the moment,' she said. 'You like spontaneity.'

He felt the edge of spontaneity now, heaven help him. 'And you don't?'

'Not…often. No.' She coloured slightly. 'Are you going to keep your vow?'

'I keep my word. Yes. I'm allowed one woman for the duration.'

'*Allowed* one woman,' she echoed. 'Gosh, how magnanimous of you. It's just so marvellous that one lucky female doesn't get to miss out on your attentions.'

He laughed lightly at her false gushiness. She was right, of course, it was ridiculous. 'Glad you agree given the female is you.'

'What?'

'We slept together after the timer had started.'

She stared at him. 'Which means…'

'Which means you're the only woman I'll be sleeping with for the next two months.'

She just kept staring at him.

He leaned forward and waved a hand in front of her eyes. 'Why, Skylar, are you so ecstatic that you've gone catatonic?'

She finally blinked. 'What if I don't want to sleep with you?'

His smile widened. 'Oh, sweetheart, we both know that's not the case.'

Her whole face radiated irritation. 'You're the most arrogant prat on the face of the earth.'

'Yeah, but you still want me. You like what I do to you,' he said boldly. 'I mean, you gave me your virginity in less than twenty minutes.'

And how *that* was possible he was still trying to figure out. This was Skylar—passionate, fiery Skylar. How had she gone all this time without sex?

'We've already established that I wasn't thinking at the time.'

'And who's to say there won't be another incident where you find yourself "not thinking"?'

'Me,' she said. 'I'm here to say there won't.' She folded her arms and glared at him. 'I enjoyed myself. But I don't actually like you.'

He shrugged. 'Who needs like when there's lust?'

'Not happening.'

But she was flushed and he was so drawn to her flame.

He'd meant to play this stupid bet out slow. Find someone suitable who he could trust to play it discreetly with him. No one had seen him with Skylar tonight, so in theory he could ask her to keep this quiet and still make an arrangement with someone else as he'd originally intended. But he couldn't lie. He wanted to win honestly. Which meant he was stuck with her. And that wasn't quite as terrible as he'd first thought. Because her reactions to him now were endlessly entertaining.

So this had just become a game within a game.

He knew she was a pleaser and insanely loyal—to everyone but him, that was. So he was going to have to convince her by some other means.

'It's not looking good for you, is it?' she said. 'Less than a day since you made your stupid bet.'

'You think I can't control myself?'

'Obviously not,' she said drolly. 'I'm astonished you suggested this when they'll all think you're the one least likely to succeed...' She squinted. 'Which was the point for you. Proving people wrong.'

'You're right.' He aimed for contrition. 'I really need your help.'

She shot him the most deadly look ever. 'You're asking for my help now?'

He couldn't resist aggravating her. Apparently it was an uncontrollable urge where she was concerned. 'If I'm seen with you, then that will stop other women from approaching me.'

'Is that a problem for you?'

'That article has had an impact already. Many messages.'

'How *awful*.' She pressed her hand to her chest in a gesture of mock empathy.

'I know. Would you believe I've even been stalked at a party? This random woman was lurking in my private garden pretending to be caught on a tree branch.'

'Really.' She gritted her teeth. 'So now you want us to fake date?'

'No. You can just be my personal bodyguard. Protect me from the *other* bodies. We don't have to hold hands or kiss in public or anything. It can be purely platonic if you want.'

She stared at him like he was nuts. Which he was.

'Can't you just not go out? You can't possibly stay at home?' she asked. 'Not date at all? Be single like a normal person?'

'I don't think so, no.' There seriously was a bunch of messages. Not that he'd prove it to her, because she'd accuse him of arrogance all over again, and he needed a break from the salty edge of her tongue. Otherwise, he'd end up silencing her with his, and that would be unwise. 'Don't worry. I won't do anything you don't want me to,' he assured her. 'People will see us and assume what they want to assume. It's usually the worst. Or the best, depending on your perspective. Whatever. It'll keep the heat off me.'

Skylar tried to calm down, not be stupidly flattered and actually say yes. This whole thing was vintage Zane deMarco outrageousness. 'This is all about you. What's in it for me?'

His smile came slow and wicked. 'Whatever you want.'

'Well now, there's an offer.' She paused for dramatic effect then batted her lashes at him. 'Back off Helberg.'

'Anything but *that*.' He shook his head. 'No point in the bet at all if I just give it up because you asked.' He stepped closer. 'Seeing you're still working for Helberg and they're obviously not paying you enough, I'll pay you.'

'I do *not* want your money,' she said stiffly.

He chuckled. Of course he'd only offered that to wind her up.

'I'm a danger to you,' she said softly. 'If they found out about this…' She began to smile. 'You *need* me.'

He stiffened. 'I don't *need* anyone.'

'Well, I certainly don't *need* to help you. Surely I'm better off seeing you date other people so either Cade or Adam could win. They might have better plans for Helberg.'

A fiery glint lit his eyes. 'They'll be *vastly* worse.'

She'd waved a red rag in front of a bull and it felt good.

He was a danger to *her*. She just had to play this game well. She felt a shiver of anticipation at the prospect of pitting her wits against his.

'Better the devil you know, surely. And you do know me.' He paused and added softly, 'Even better now.'

Well, she definitely knew him better than she knew either Cade or Adam or indeed any other man. And he was too close again. Making her brain operate too slowly. 'I want time.'

He nodded, coming closer still. 'For what?'

'Not that,' she muttered. She was not sleeping with him again. That had been a mistake. A marvellous but utterly unrepeatable mistake.

'Then for what?' he asked innocently.

'I want to show you Helberg. What it was, what it is and what it could be.'

'Like the Ghost of Christmas Past?' He shook his head slowly. 'You want to humanise me? Too late, Skylar.'

She held firm. 'Time.'

'You do realise that I'll use everything you show me as part of my acquisition preparation.'

'Of course you will, but I don't consider it a risk because I won't be showing you anything confidential. But I'll get you inside the company corridors, which is closer than you've been in a while, right?'

His expression shuttered. 'Skylar—'

'Don't patronise me.' She stood in front of him. 'You break companies up.'

'Yes. So they survive in some form.'

'Do they, though?' she challenged. 'More often than

not companies go under once they've been stripped of their assets.'

'Helberg is old and unwieldy. Reed overstretched and his model is no longer commercially viable. Think of it as lifesaving surgery. We cut out the rot—the parts of the company not performing.'

'And sell that rot to someone else?'

'Sure. One person's rot is another person's treasure...'

'And a guy like you gets rich on the quick sale. But you leave little more than a skeleton that has no chance of long-term survival.' She lifted her chin. 'I think I can prove to you that it's a company worth holding together.'

Her loyalty meant she couldn't stand by and see it destroyed. Because of her colleagues and the values the company had stood for. Helberg had done good for others for generations. Now she had nothing left to lose and she had to try. Was he as soulless as she'd thought—or was there an echo of that kind boy who'd shared his candy with a crying kid still inside him?

But he was still. Silent. Unemotional. Uncaring.

Skylar's heart sank. She had no chance of convincing either Cade or Adam given she didn't even know them. So in spite of everything, Zane was actually *her* best bet. She needed *him* to win, so she would help him.

She straightened. 'I'll be seen with you once a week so you still have a chance with your stupid bet. In return, once a week, you come with me on a visit to Helberg. That's my offer. Take it or leave it.'

He didn't answer. Still didn't move. But she saw the flicker in his eyes.

'Come to the office next week,' she said. 'I'll text you with a time that's convenient.'

'What if it's not convenient for me?' he muttered huskily.

She shrugged. 'It's your choice. You want to be seen with me then you'll make it convenient. I'm not the one trapped in a stupid bet.'

'You know you won't change my mind, Skylar.'

Probably not, but she had to try. And she grudgingly respected that he was trying to warn her. But she had an in with him, and one thing that Skylar had always had was hope. So she smiled at him. 'We'll see, won't we?'

CHAPTER SEVEN

At 8:00 a.m. on Monday, Zane deMarco finally admitted
he had a productivity problem. The concentration catastrophe otherwise known as Skylar Bennet was lodged in his
head—in his body too—hell, she'd seemingly invaded him
on a cellular level and he had so *many* questions.

Not that any of the answers were truly his business. He
shouldn't be distracted by Skylar Bennet's lack of a sex life.
He should be more concerned by his *own* complete loss of
control. The smile she'd shot him when she'd realised she
had a little power? The dimple had surfaced and he'd had
to summon every ounce of restraint not to lose it and haul
her straight back into his arms.

He had fun with his lovers, yes, but he'd never been in
an incident where the drive to have a woman had been so
overpowering. Okay, he'd felt it one other time. With her.
Which was deeply annoying. And this had only happened
now because of that back then, right? It was some sort of
warped want for the one he'd been told he couldn't have.

He'd barely slept on Saturday night. Sure, he slept badly
at the best of times, sometimes troubled by twinges in his
leg, sometimes just restless as hell. But knowing she was
under the same roof had rendered sleep impossible. For

hours he'd battled the urge to stalk to her bedroom. Hours cursing himself for his impatience.

He'd taken her too fast and it had been over too soon.

Sunday morning had been nothing short of awkward, which frankly was another foreign situation. Usually he'd slide from a one-nighter by sending them off with his chauffeur and a smile. But yesterday he'd driven Skylar himself. He'd taken her to the small motel so she could collect her things, then insisted she share his helicopter back to Manhattan. He couldn't watch her board that painfully slow bus. Once they'd made it back to the city, he'd insisted on driving her to her apartment. And yeah, it'd been entirely to suit his own ends. He'd wanted to know where she lived. He'd wanted to extend the time they shared even though it was torture. And the fact that she'd so clearly wanted to *refuse* all those offers had been deliciously amusing. Because she knew that he'd seen her reluctance—and so she'd accepted his offer at every turn. Which was even more delicious torture. They'd barely spoken. She'd appeared lost in thought. He'd just been battling his incredibly basic urges. The hottest of highlights from those moments in the orchard had flicked through his mind the whole time. Even now, only one thought in five was actually relevant to business; the rest were not safe for work.

It was also because of that stupid bet, right?

Cursing the whole stupid idea, he went online and skimmed the magazine and saw there was an update to the article already. They'd loaded a photo of Adam taken only last night. And they'd added a *tally*.

It looked a typical Courtney Collection event—glamorous and elite, and Adam was with society model Annabel St James no less. Zane copied the picture into a text and tapped out a quick caption.

Could do worse for the summer! ;)

He winced at the weak banter but he was incapable of coming up with anything better. Grimly he realised the poll that had been started was the worst thing possible. Was *any* photo of him standing next to any woman going to count? Surely not. He glanced at the photo of Adam— there was clear contact between the man and his date. There was nothing on Cade yet. Nothing on Zane either, but that wasn't surprising. Danielle's Independence Day party was renowned for its privacy protections for her guests.

Why had he told Skylar about the bet? Pillow talk totally wasn't his thing. But he'd enjoyed being brutally honest with her—and he'd wanted to shock her. Because she'd shocked him. But no one knew about the bet other than Adam and Cade. Skylar could make them far more of a laughing stock than the original article had if she went public. Which meant he was forced to keep her close.

Anticipation tore through him. He could keep her very close. He could turn that judgment in her eyes to surrender again. Because her judgment pinched in a way that the judgment of anyone else didn't. Maybe it was because she knew the shitty apartment building he'd grown up in, the underfunded school. Because it had been her building, her school too…

She knew more about him than almost anyone—despite the fact that in all those years they'd spoken only a handful of times.

But she'd also betrayed him. That one time they'd touched, they'd been caught and she'd let him take the blame. So of all people not to give a damn about, Skylar ought to be top of his list. And he didn't give a damn, he just wanted…what? Aside from the obvious.

He wanted a little *honesty*.

She'd said she didn't want to have sex with him again but that wasn't true. He'd bet that when it came to it, she wouldn't be able to control herself any more than he could. But she didn't *want* to want him. Which was different. So he'd respect her rule. If he had to be celibate for the rest of the summer, he would. Purely to confound her. Even if it was going to kill him.

But he'd torment her in other ways. He'd spar with her. Provoke her. Because when he didn't hold back, she bit. *That's* how she was different now. She wasn't silently watching any more. She snapped back. He wanted more and that he *could* have. Hell, maybe he'd even provoke her sensuality—just a little. But even so, what little honour remained in him dictated he be honest about his intentions regarding Helberg. He'd told her up front that her plan was going to fail. Apparently that wasn't going to stop her from trying. Though if she thought he was going to sit around waiting for her summons, she had another thing coming.

Zane didn't wait for anyone any more. Certainly not Skylar Bennet. He'd done that once before, and he wasn't being burned by her again.

He cleared his schedule, cancelled meetings and postponed delivery dates for reports from his stunned underlings.

At nine on Monday morning, Zane deMarco walked through the atrium of Helberg Holdings and threw the blinking receptionist a wide smile.

'I'm here to see Skylar Bennet,' he said suavely. 'She's expecting me.'

* * *

Skylar's jaw ached from gritting her teeth so hard in the ten seconds it took for the elevator to take her from the fifth floor down to the atrium.

He was here. Unexpected. Uninvited. Wasn't that just typical of the man, to try to throw her off her game?

She was already off. She'd barely slept in the last forty-eight hours as she'd struggled to process what she'd done with Zane. And the only regret she could summon was that it had been only the once.

She was angrier than ever with him. Why him? Why *only* him? It was a chemical catastrophe. Why hadn't she met anyone else she wanted any of that with? It was horrifically unfair.

Because it had been so, so good and it was all she could think about. The delicious aches in her body reminded her with every step of the intimacy, and heaven help her, all she wanted was a repeat. With *him*. Which was appalling. She hated him. They were polar opposites and they wanted wildly different things. And she'd gone her whole life without needing sex so why did she have all these nymphomaniac urges now?

Because it had been so, so good.

But after that shocking conversation when he'd told her about that *bet*, he'd politely led her back to that immaculate bedroom with its enormous beautiful bed. That she'd not slept a wink in. The next morning, he'd offered her a stunning breakfast of French pastries and fruit. She'd opted for black coffee. He'd stuck by her side all the way back to Manhattan and she'd struggled to stay calm the entire time. Her nervous system was caught in a cycle of chaos. It was the most appalling attraction. But thank goodness she'd had enough nous to block any idea of them sleeping together again, because *he* clearly wasn't interested in anything more than her 'help' in winning that ridiculous bet. She shouldn't have offered to assist him. She should've left him to stew in his mess. She should tell that magazine about their outrageousness and humiliate them all.

The problem was Helberg. It was more than her job—it was her whole life. Yes, as a student, it had been her safe place—she'd interned in the various departments during her varsity holidays. Then she'd come to live and work full-time in Manhattan. She'd worked *hard*. Her father had been so proud and she'd begun saving to get him into a better home—because he'd worked hard for her for years. She'd slowly got to know some colleagues, cared about them. And she'd kept working hard—because that's what you had to do to remain valued. Needed. Wanted.

When her father had passed, she'd buried herself deeper in her work. It was what he'd have wanted. He'd be devastated to see the company go under. She had nothing much outside of it. So she had to stop it from happening. And Zane was her one and only access point to the elite power brokers.

She spotted him the second the elevator doors slid open. Hard to miss him given he was leaning against the pillar opposite and looking appallingly gorgeous. Apparently he'd slept well, given he was such a vision of vitality. That charming smile curved his lips but the ice blue eyes were sharp. Her nerves tightened. Her lower belly basically burst into flames.

She gritted her teeth harder, feeling as if she'd just run down the twenty flights of stairs instead of taking the lift. It took everything to keep her chin up and her gaze locked on him as she walked over.

'What are you doing here?' she asked through a forced smile, aware that everyone in the atrium was watching.

He straightened and stepped closer, staring right into her eyes, and his smile deepened in intimacy. 'You promised to show me *everything*.'

Skylar stalled, needing a second to snatch a breath. His ability to imply innuendo in every other comment was impressive. And annoying. Because for all that huskiness, he didn't mean it. He truly was a one-date wonder.

'I told you I'd text you a suitable time,' she said crisply.

'I didn't get where I am today by waiting—'

'No,' she interrupted firmly. 'You just turn up when *you* like and take what *you* want.'

He cocked his head ever so slightly and that arrogant charm lit his eyes, but she was determined not to be swayed by it.

'I apologise for misunderstanding.' His smile was shamelessly *un*apologetic. 'Naturally I assumed you'd mean first thing Monday morning given saving Helberg from my evil plans is surely your highest priority.'

'Right.'

He leaned close—too close—and dropped his voice even lower. 'Saturday night for our date, by the way. I'll pick you up from your apartment. I have the address locked in.'

Skylar was aware of the receptionist hovering—watching, listening—and the other people in the atrium all not-so-surreptitiously staring. She needed to get him somewhere private because he was putting on a show. She just needed to remember that it *was* a show and there was no need for her body to react as if his flirtations were real.

'Of course.' She held her stance and smiled super politely. 'If you'll follow me.'

'Gladly,' he said so meekly that she just glared at him.

He remained silent in the elevator while she was too steamed to speak. She briskly walked to one of the meeting rooms on the executive floor. A million people milled in the corridor. Yes, word was out and everyone was out to see for themselves that Zane deMarco was here. And definitely wondering why. Hopefully her boss wasn't going to ask any difficult questions later. The perils of her plan presented themselves in rapid succession. She would never show Zane anything commercially sensitive—never jeopardise her own career or Helberg's reputation. Plus regulatory bodies might get involved—their bet was dodgy enough, surely?

'Second thoughts, Skylar?' he murmured as she closed the door behind him.

How could he read her mind?

'Don't worry.' He dominated the space in the room. 'I won't ask you to do anything you're uncomfortable with.'

Her body heated even more. More innuendo that he probably didn't mean. He was only out to tip her off balance. He talked up a game, but he wasn't really playing. His desire for Helberg was no joke.

'What's your role here these days?' he asked.

'People and culture.'

'HR? You?'

His obvious surprise annoyed her. 'You think I'm not good with people?'

He definitely wanted to throw her off but she wasn't going to let him. In fact, she was going to make him pay for his arrogance and entitlement. He really assumed she'd drop everything to accommodate him. The man needed a lesson. He was about to get it.

She smiled at him. 'If you'll wait here a moment, I'll make arrangements for this morning's information session.'

His eyes widened. 'Sure.'

She left him in the room and stalked to her own office. She couldn't believe he wanted to break up a massive company with such a prestigious history. The Helberg brand had been around for more than a century and was renowned. The dynasty had engaged in a wide variety of philanthropic endeavours in many ways. But yes, in recent years, some of Reed Helberg's decisions had raised questions in the boardroom. Some divisions had struggled. But that was still no reason to break it up completely.

Zane deMarco just had a thing for a sledgehammer. She couldn't understand how he could so easily destroy what others had taken so long to build. Why didn't he respect their effort? She needed to show him some of the people he'd be hurting.

She picked up her phone. Three minutes later, she went back into the meeting room. As she approached, she noted his was expression was cool but his gaze watchful. She couldn't resist stepping just a little too close—as he'd done to her. It was an absurdly strong satisfaction when he tensed and she heard his sharp intake of breath.

'Bernie is going to show you from the ground level the kind of systems Helberg has,' she said.

'Systems?'

'Heating and ventilation, sprinkler systems.'

He took a beat. 'Are you talking about building main-tenance?'

'Helberg constructs and services all its own buildings.' She smiled at him. 'Here's Bernie now.'

Bernie was almost seventy. Super hardworking and loyal and he refused to retire. He was damned good at his job. And he was talkative. Very talkative. A fact she appreciated. She didn't think Zane would.

'If you'll come with me, Mr deMarco,' Bernie said jovially.

She saw Zane's mouth thin but he didn't demur. It was only when Skylar didn't move with them that he turned back to her.

'Are you not coming on the tour, Skylar?' he asked silkily.

'Sadly I've another appointment.'

'More important than me?'

She simply smiled.

Three hours later, she paced the meeting room back and forth and back and forth. What was taking so long? She'd expected Bernie to keep him busy for a while, but not for *this* amount of time. It was the worst idea she'd ever had. She hadn't got any work done herself and she'd probably have infuriated him with this time waster of a meeting. Yet she couldn't help inwardly chuckling at the thought of immaculately suited and booted Zane wandering through the pump room and maintenance tunnels.

Maybe he'd left the building without saying goodbye—given up on the whole thing. Disappointment hit hard at that thought—she wanted that date more than she was willing to admit. She was weak.

Half an hour later she swallowed her pride and went down to the basement to investigate what had happened. Bernie's office door was wide open and she heard voices, then laughter. Stepping through, she saw the old man was leaning back in his chair, beaming, and there were take-out coffee cups and bagel and donut wrappers littering the desk. Skylar's mouth watered. Zane was in the seat beside Bernie—he'd pulled it round so the two men were side by side. He'd removed his jacket and tie and his sleeves were rolled up and she couldn't stand to look at his arms. Like Bernie, he was laughing.

He glanced up as she appeared and his gaze brightened. 'Oh, Skylar!' He smiled at her wickedly and raised his half-eaten donut to her in a mock salute. 'Were you waiting for us? Have Bernie and I lost track of time?'

'A little.' She smiled through gritted teeth. 'It's probably time we let Bernie get back to it, I'm sure he has things he needs to attend to—'

'Not at all,' Bernie interjected. 'It's been a pleasure to have you here, Zane. Come back anytime.'

'Thanks, Bernie.' Zane shot Skylar a sideways look. 'I'll be sure to do that.'

Oh, *please*. Skylar watched as Zane took his time to stand and take his jacket from the back of the chair. He and Bernie shook hands and Zane was intolerably genuine in his thanks. Of course Zane had charmed the man and now they were BFFs for life.

Turning, he licked a little sugar from his lip and batted his lashes at her. 'Where next, Skylar?'

'I'll see you to reception,' Skylar muttered.

'Afraid I won't find my way on my own?' His smile widened. 'You trust me that little?'

She pushed open the door to the stairwell. It was one flight of stairs. *One*. But as she got to the landing, Zane stopped two steps below her.

'Is something wrong?' she asked when he didn't move.

He was looking directly into her eyes. She should have taken him to the elevator.

'I'm curious. Do you really believe that that experience would make me want to keep this company intact?'

That 'experience'? She frowned and moved to the edge of the top step to see his expression. Had he been faking that friendliness with Bernie? Good to know. But she was disappointed in him. 'Wasn't it worth your precious time?'

she asked sarcastically. 'Well, too bad. You deserved it because you don't value other people's time. I figured why not waste some of yours?'

'I value your time,' he said softly. 'Most of all I value the time we *share*, together.'

Every muscle tensed. She was *not* going to be taken in by him. 'Does that sort of line actually work?'

But she was flustered. *Really* flustered.

'It's not a line,' he said simply. 'It's the truth.'

'Stop—'

'And you're wrong, by the way,' he interrupted. '*I'm* not the one wasting my time here. This morning's session with Bernie was extremely worthwhile. He's a very nice guy.'

That disappointment melted and she softened towards him. 'Yes. I'd trust him with my life. He's been here for ever.'

'Yeah.' He climbed one step so he was closer. 'He told me a lot about you.'

'He…*what*?' Skylar's breath stalled. 'What did he tell you?'

'Lots. You're first in, last out. You know everyone by name—'

'I work in HR. It would be bad if I didn't—'

'Care too much? I really don't get why you're still working here,' he said. 'You're bright. You work hard. You could've been VP at some other company already. Instead you're side-tracked taking on all the projects no one else wants. Bernie said you leap to help anyone who asks. That it's too easy for you to say yes and you find it impossible to say no. Which is so ironic when apparently it's the reverse in the rest of your life.'

She gaped.

'Do you still feel like you owe the company something?' he pressed her. 'Loyalty can last only so long. You should have moved on right after your internship. This company is merely a machine that will chew you up till there's nothing left. It doesn't value *you*.'

'You're wrong,' she whispered.

'I think you already know I'm not.' He lifted her braid and resettled it over her shoulder.

'Don't toy with me,' she whispered.

'Is that what you think I'm doing?' He shook his head and smiled. 'You're the one who won't let me get past on the stairs. *You're* the one standing too close...'

She mirrored his gentle shake of the head. 'You're the one inappropriately touching me. Go find someone else to sleep with.'

'Can't. You know I've made a vow not to sleep around for a couple of months.'

'I still can't fathom why you'd suggest something so obviously counter to your nature,' she muttered tartly. 'Sleeping around is as essential to your existence as breathing.'

He put his hand around her waist and pulled so she almost teetered on the edge of the top step. 'Go harder on me,' he smiled wolfishly. 'I like it when you don't hold back. Just be prepared for the same in return.'

It was dynamite again. And yes—she wanted to best him in so many ways.

A door slammed in the stairwell above them. Skylar stepped back at the same time as he dropped his arm. She stalked ahead, leading him back into the atrium but super aware of how close he was behind her and how much she'd wanted him closer still.

'You've played your first card regarding Helberg, time to pay up with a *very* high-profile date,' he said calmly. 'Be ready.'

'How formal?' she choked.

'I'll be in black tie.'

So she was going to need a dress. Not slinky. Not white. She'd find something that covered her from top to toe. An enormous sack, perhaps.

Thankfully the atrium was emptier than it had been when he'd arrived this morning. She saw him glance up at the large portrait of Reed Helberg that hung above the exit and his smile evaporated.

'You okay?' she asked curiously.

He stiffened. 'Of course.'

She didn't believe him. 'You never liked him. Why?'

He kept his gaze on the painting. 'What makes you think that?'

'You clashed the night you came back and did that speech at school.' The night he'd told her she was pathetic. 'Something must have happened to make you want to destroy his legacy so badly.'

'This isn't revenge, Skylar,' he scoffed, but his smile didn't reach his eyes. 'This is just business. Their numbers no longer add up—surely you've looked, you must see it. Nothing lasts. Not even old money.'

No, judging by the look in his eyes a second ago, there was more to it than that. 'You don't care what others think *now*, but I think you cared about *him*. About what *he* thought.'

He remained silent, his expression blank. But for once that told her something. Adrenalin pooled inside her as she realised she was right. 'How you feel about Helberg—about Reed—is *personal*. He's different.'

And if she could understand what it was that bothered Zane about Reed, then she might be able to find a solution—an alternative ending to the one he was pushing for.

But Zane wasn't looking at the portrait any more. He was looking at her.

'Why do you look so pleased about that?' he growled.

'Because it shows someone can get through your defences.' Her heart pounded but she couldn't help but be honest with him. 'Someone can actually get to you.'

His lips twisted into a rueful smile. 'No, Skylar.'

'No?' It didn't look that way to her.

'Not any more,' he added softly.

But someone once had—*Helberg*. How and in what way? He clearly wasn't about to tell her, which also meant that Zane still felt strongly about him. And in turn, that meant he still *felt*, full stop. So maybe she had more of a chance than she'd originally thought, because there was something of a heart still inside him.

'I think I can make you change your mind,' she whispered.

'It's a good thing you've got time to adjust to failure.' Zane brushed her cheekbone with the lightest stroke of his fingertip. 'You won't take it so hard.'

CHAPTER EIGHT

ZANE STRAIGHTENED HIS TIE, swept his hand through his hair and stalked out to the waiting car. He'd been irritable all week. The days had dragged as he'd gone straight from home to work and back again, not setting a foot anywhere else so he wouldn't inadvertently be 'seen' with someone. He'd been counting down the hours until he got his driver to take him back to her apartment. Skylar Bennet was still a catastrophe.

'Take a couple turns around the block,' he muttered to his driver when he paused outside her apartment building. 'I'll message when ready.'

His muscles twitched. He'd run up all seventy-odd stairs in his condo tower earlier today but even that hadn't been enough to use up his excess energy.

He pushed the button and she buzzed him up. By the time he'd climbed to the second floor she'd opened her door and was visible in the frame. For the first time all week, he stood stock still.

'Is this on the mark?' She sounded nervous but looked defiant.

Oh, it was on the mark. Very, *very* on the mark—if the mark was his libido. The silver slip dress skimmed her slim frame. Her glossy hair fell sleekly to the curve of her bottom. Her skin was radiant and those deep brown eyes of hers were huge. 'I've worn heels so I won't look stupidly short next to you.'

He liked her height. He remembered pressing her against him in the garden and wrapping her leg around his waist. He wanted that again.

She frowned in the face of his silence. 'I rented a couple alternatives if it isn't…'

He struggled to rein in the direction of his thoughts. 'How very diligent of you, Skylar.'

'I like to do a good job.' She straightened.

'I know you do.' He stepped past her into her apartment. That she thought of this as a 'job' irritated him. 'We're going to a film premiere. A thriller, I believe. You can hold my hand in the scary bits if you like.'

He moved deeper into her apartment and discovered it was tiny. Which was a problem. He couldn't trust himself to touch her—not even offering a socially polite kiss on her cheek. Getting that close to her was impossible—he actually feared he'd lose control and caveman toss her onto her own bed. He'd take her fully clothed first, then he'd rip the beautiful dress from her and have her all over again. Naked. And then again. And yes, he was going out of his mind.

'There'll be lots of cameras at a film premiere.' She closed the door behind him.

'Yes. We'll walk the red carpet. Pose in front of the press pen.'

'Press pen?' She sounded aghast. 'You're kidding.'

He focused on the apartment. The absolute lack of space. There wasn't even a kitchen. Just a sink and a microwave.

Her low mumble reached him. 'What's the worst they're going to say…' she muttered. 'Probably that I'm not pretty enough to be seen with you.'

He turned.

'And that I'm not from the right sort of society.' She fiddled with the strap of her purse. 'Will they pry into my past? How detail oriented are these people?'

Very, unfortunately. He had a lot of money and stupidly that made people interested.

'You want to back out, Skylar?' he asked, though he really didn't want to.

'Not at all. I can handle this.' But she didn't look as certain as she sounded. 'It's not like I have a past to be worried about.'

'If you worry what someone thinks, that gives them power over you. You get distracted wondering about their reactions, which means you can't make a clean decision on your own. Like your dress tonight. No one else's opinion should matter. Only yours. If you're comfortable, if you like the dress—'

'So not even your opinion matters?' she interrupted.

'No. It doesn't.'

She cared too much. Always had. Seeking approval. He remembered her silence. Her dutiful manner to her father. And he was suddenly reluctant to expose her to that online commentary. The magazine was bad enough, but worse were those trolls who hid behind anonymous screens and keyboards and spouted cruel words for the malevolent fun of it. The thought of them had never bothered him before but now he was concerned for her sake. She was about to lose her privacy—paying a steep price for what? Nothing. Because there was *zero* chance of him changing his mind on breaking up Helberg. A bitter taste rose in the back of his throat. *Guilt.* But he couldn't tell her what had really happened between him and Helberg and the immediate aftermath of that excruciating meeting when he'd been a child. He'd never spoken of it—or of the accident after—with anyone. Not even his mother. He kept that shit well buried where it couldn't bother him and it would never see the light of day.

But here she was, wondering why he wanted Helberg so much. Acute enough to know there was something more than business about it. And perhaps he could explain just *some* of it. Because there was that greedy part of him, the part that liked to win. That part didn't want to quit this game. Not yet. Besides which, he reassured himself, she looked stunning. No online troll could ever say otherwise. 'Skylar, you could wear anything and—'

'Please don't flatter—'

'I'm *not*.' He gritted his teeth to stop himself *showing* rather than telling her how much of a freaking goddess she was. 'You're beautiful. Your dress showcases the fact.'

'I thought you didn't like me.'

'Right. But I still think you're sexy.'

There were two other dresses hanging from the door that he presumed led to the bathroom. One was midnight blue, the other was short and a bold red. His mouth dried. He wanted to see her in both. Yeah, he'd suddenly turned into some warlord who wanted his woman to try them on and twirl before him. He'd sit on that too-small sofa, legs sprawled apart, hard as a rock, and watch her like some totally erotic movie montage moment. That was *definitely* the premiere he'd prefer tonight.

'We should go.' She snapped her clutch purse. 'My apartment isn't really big enough for us both.'

He forced a smile. 'You don't want to move somewhere a little bigger?'

'It's close to work.'

Which was seemingly her one and only priority. His irritation resurged. 'And that's all that matters?'

Why did she still work there like a loyal little angel full of optimism and misplaced hope? Because she liked the people she worked with. That had been the main thing he'd learned from Bernie. Her loyalty to them—the way she went the extra mile. Didn't say no. Still a pleaser then—to those she felt she owed or something. Irritation rippled. She shouldn't spend her life repaying debts no one else bothered with. Why waste her time when it was clearly crumbling? She was good. She knew her numbers. Surely she could recognise that it was too late to turn that massive ship around. The iceberg was imminent and Helberg was going to sink.

'It's close to some good restaurants too,' she said.

'Oh?' He watched her sceptically. She wouldn't go to any. He bet she started early at the office and stayed late and probably lived on snacks and cereal.

'Yes, I have a good relationship with the Thai restaurant one block over. They deliver.'

Deliver. Right.

She tilted her chin at him. 'It's close to the park too.'

Yeah, he'd noticed the worn shoes at the front door. 'You still run?'

She nodded, colour rising in her cheeks. The room went silent. She was remembering that morning. Same as him. He couldn't ask her about it. Couldn't think about it.

'Every day.' She cleared her throat. 'And a group run on Saturdays.'

'Such a strict schedule,' he teased weakly. 'No such thing as spontaneity in your life—'

'That was last week.'

And never to be repeated. Yeah, he got it. He forced

himself to look away from her again. It was a petite apartment for a petite person and perfectly set up just for her. Everything was neat and just so. Her bed was on a mezzanine level with the lowest of ceilings so he'd hit his head if he were up there and on top—

He tore his gaze away, not letting himself finish that thought. 'You're right, we really should go.'

Unfortunately the drive didn't take all that long.

'Right...' Skylar drew in a steadying breath as they approached the theatre. 'You need me to smile? Look adoringly at you?'

Her speech had quickened, risen. She was nervous. He hadn't seen her at parties in all these years. He got that she hadn't gone out when she was young because of her father, but why hadn't she since she'd left home? Why still so very alone and seemingly isolated aside from work friends—at least one of whom was almost three times her age?

He didn't want her 'performing' to any script of his. Didn't want to have any control over what she did...though of course he'd made her come here tonight with him, hadn't he?

'You never have to smile,' he said shortly. 'Not if you don't want to. Look as moody as you like. I'm not asking you to fake anything for me. Tonight we're merely companions.'

But that wasn't entirely true. They were enemies. With chemistry.

The red carpet walk wasn't long but it was crowded. In the photo pen ahead the photographers were calling loudly to the film stars.

'What do you think of the hero?' He jerked his chin towards the buff guy posing with quite a stunning selection of angular jaw expressions.

'Gonna ditch me for him if you get the chance?' He

was half curious as to whether the blond Adonis type was for her.

She rose on tiptoe to study the actor for a moment and Zane actually felt a stab of—

'Maybe...' She turned and lifted her face to his, batting her lashes coyly.

'Don't believe you,' he whispered in her ear. 'He's not arrogant enough for you.'

That dimple appeared and then her giggle sounded. 'True.'

He couldn't wipe the smile from his own face. He pulled her close to guide her through the crowd. And then, greedy man that he was, he kept his arm around her, faking nothing.

He had no idea what happened in the movie. He was too distracted thinking about her. Smelling the soft scent of her hair. As the house lights came on in the theatre, he wrapped his arm around her waist again—purely to guide her back through those crowds again.

'What now?' she asked quietly. 'Is there an after party?'

'Yes. You want to go to it?'

Skylar hesitated, unsure how to answer. She didn't want this night to end, but she didn't want to be around all those other people and have everyone watching because she didn't want their physical contact to be purely performative. 'Do you?'

'I'm not saying.' He shot her a tantalising smile. 'I dare *you* to make the decision, Skylar. You don't need to please me or answer however you think that I want you to. Do what *you* want.'

Her pulse quickened. He'd *dared* her again. She was sure it was deliberate. Because that day her father had demanded the opposite over and over again—*Don't you dare...*

What she *wanted* was to be alone with him. They'd not had enough time alone *together*. Belatedly she realised that this movie was his version of Bernie. The lack of time together *alone* was a deliberate choice. This really was only about being seen with the same woman in public. He wouldn't be with her at all if it weren't for that stupid bet of his. He'd had his actual 'one-date wonder' with her and this was only for show.

'I was merely being polite,' she muttered. 'These dates are your nights and what we do on them is your call.'

He stared down at her and that intensity in his eyes sharpened. She couldn't move as she replayed her own tragic innuendo again. It'd honestly just slipped out—as if her subconscious determinedly sent him the invitation before she could think. But his wordless response—just that look in his eyes—made her toes curl.

Only he said nothing. He was good at that when he wanted to be. Saying nothing and walking away.

'I should go home.' But she ached for an alternative. And then she was mortified to be so bowled over by the charm he turned on anyone at any time.

He pulled his phone from his jacket pocket. 'I'll call the car.'

He kept his phone out and scrolled through some messages on the drive. She had little to say anyway, too busy battling her disappointment at his easy acquiescence.

Stupid hormones. They'd been triggered by their one-night stand last week and she needed to turn them back off. Urgently. She thought about the guys at university she'd kissed. The invitations at work that she'd turned down. People had stopped asking. Probably said she was frigid and honestly she was glad. It had made it easier. She'd wanted to focus only on work. And she had. Until now. Anger bubbled inside of her. But it wasn't just that—hunger clawed. That old drive to be near *him*. Life was cruel. Why was it that the one guy who turned her on was an irritating play-boy who only wanted one woman once?

Finally his driver pulled up outside her apartment and she forced a polite farewell for Zane. 'Thanks for tonight, I enjoyed it more than I thought I would.'

His sardonic smile flashed. 'Even the press pen?'

'Oh, no, that was hideous. I probably have my eyes closed in every photo.'

'You don't.' He held up his phone to her.

'They're out there already?' She leaned closer to study the pictures. For a moment she was stunned. Her eyes weren't closed—she was too busy gazing up at him. It made her wince. This 'date' *was* fake, but her interest in him couldn't be more obvious. She channelled her embar-rassment into annoyance. 'Don't you *hate* this? It's such an invasion of your privacy.'

'Generally I don't bother looking. It's meaningless. But in this case, it's how I'm going to win that bet.'

The damned bet. Helberg, the reason for it all. 'Why do you want Helberg so badly? I don't believe you'd make such a sacrifice for just *any* company—'

'You think my spending time with you is some kind of a sacrifice?' he interrupted, the pale blue of his eyes sud-denly fiery.

She froze, caught in the flames.

'Did you know you have this cute dimple in your left cheek?' he said quietly. 'See it here?' He pointed to one of the pictures. 'It doesn't appear when you smile politely. Only when you giggle. I'm glad I made you giggle then.'

Embarrassed, she lifted her hand to her mouth.

'And your immediate response is to hide it,' he scoffed. 'Why is that?'

But *he* was the one hiding—completely avoiding answering her question about Helberg. Again. Which was infuriating.

'While your immediate response when faced with a difficult conversation is to distract your way out of it with flattery and flirtation. Or else you just go silent.' She glared up at him. 'You don't want to tell me the truth.'

He stared at her for a long moment. 'All right, I'll tell you about Reed Helberg if you answer *my* questions.'

'About what?'

He shook his head. 'That's my offer. Take it or leave it.'

'Everything is a game to you.'

'Not a game. A deal. In fact, this is a *bargain* because it's so easy. It's merely some answers to some questions—how difficult can that be?'

'Well, it seems to be very difficult for you.' She watched him suspiciously. 'You have to be honest about you and Reed.'

There was the smallest hesitation. 'Sure, I'll be honest if you are.'

Oddly enough, she actually enjoyed being brutally honest with him and not bothering with the cautious politeness she always maintained around everyone else. 'Fine. Tell me what happened with Reed.' The man had a summer residence not far from the same town as them. A compound that had been in his family for generations. He liked to offer the scholarships to the kids of the local school. 'He must've thought you were amazing. Offered you the scholarship to end all scholarships.'

Zane hesitated again. Shadows flickered in his eyes and his features sharpened. That's when the penny dropped.

He'd been a student at her high school for all his schooling years. She'd assumed it was because of his injuries—he'd needed to remain at home. And then he'd not gone on to university because he'd already made his fortune.

'Didn't he offer you one?' she whispered.

'Clever, Skylar,' he muttered steadily. 'I wasn't good enough.'

Never could *that* be true. Never ever. Zane was a genius. And he'd had that shocking injury in the car accident that he'd fought back so strongly from. He'd shown strength and courage as well as intelligence. Whereas she'd worked so awfully hard just to be good enough for consideration.

'How is that possible?' she asked.

He chuckled but the bitterness touched her. 'I guess I wasn't the right kind of polite, malleable student who he could wheel out in front of guests to make him look good. He was pure egotist.'

Malleable? Well, the last thing Zane was, was malleable. He was his own person. A maverick who seemed to take little seriously—aside from making millions. 'You were too much of a threat—'

'My own ego was,' he said. 'I made my first million when I was still at school—'

'But learning from home for half that time—'

'Right.' He blinked, disconcerted for a second. 'Fool that I was, I wanted him to admit he'd been wrong about me. I was young and egotistical enough to feel pleased about the invitation to speak at the gala but Reed couldn't have been more dismissive. Told me it was easy enough to make money. The real test was whether I'd be able to keep it. That he wasn't a betting man but he was *sure* I'd fail.'

She stilled. Reed had rejected him. Repeatedly.

But now Zane smiled in reminiscence. 'I'd had no

idea you were going to be there, but you were that year's scholar. As beautiful as ever. As well behaved as always. You wouldn't even look at me.'

She felt her skin heat. Truth was, she'd not been able to meet his eyes initially because she'd not known what to say. The last time she'd seen him had been when her father had physically pulled them apart. She'd been *mortified*. By her father. By her own silence. But Zane himself had said nothing—he'd just stalked off. And he'd stalked off from the dinner that night too. But he'd muttered as he'd passed her.

'I believe you called me pathetic,' she said.

He nodded. 'It wasn't polite of me. But you were.'

That stung. 'For being grateful?'

He drew in a deep breath.

She waited.

'It was *your* brain that got your grades,' he finally said. 'Your work. You never needed that scholarship.'

He was wrong but she couldn't tell him about the pressure her father had put on her—that both the school and varsity scholarships had provided something of a necessary escape. She felt too disloyal to her father to even think it, but sometimes she'd been caught between the contrary needs to please him and to have breathing space of her own...

'I was just someone to take your annoyance out on,' she muttered.

He shook his head. 'I was pissed off that night but even more so when I saw you.' His gaze roved over her face, settling on her eyes. 'You were the perfect little protégée.'

'We can't *all* make our first million while we're still in our teens.' She frowned, turning her thoughts back to what Zane had told her. There had to be something more personal beyond his desire to prove himself to Reed Helberg.

'Is that it?' she challenged him. 'He didn't like you, so now you want to wreck his legacy?' It didn't make sense. Not when Zane himself admitted he didn't give a damn about what anyone thought. 'I know you. *You're* not that pathetic. What aren't you telling me?'

His eyes widened. 'Those are the basic facts. Now it's my turn for questions.'

She glared at him. He glared right back. Tension pulled the silence to screaming point—until Skylar felt forced to duck his gaze.

'What do you want to know?' she growled.

'Why do you have so little fun?'

Her focus shot right back to his face. 'Fun?'

'You're twenty-six and you were a virgin. What about boyfriends?'

'Seriously?' She shot an embarrassed glance towards the driver.

'He can't hear—'

'You can ask me anything and you just want to know about my previous relationships?'

'So you've had them?' He leaned closer, eyebrows arching. 'Had they all taken a purity pledge or something?'

'There's no "they,"' she growled. 'There's been nothing and no one. Literally nothing.'

'No relationships at all?'

She shook her head.

He stilled. 'You don't go out dancing? Not to bars or parties? You're not on any dating apps?'

She kept shaking her head.

'I get that you might not want a relationship, but don't you want—?'

'Casual sex?' she interrupted. 'No.'

'Yet that's what you had with me the other night,' he muttered. 'And you enjoyed it.'

'Yes.' But she couldn't have it again. It wasn't anything like she'd thought it would be. It had been hot and intense and honestly, all the damn stars had burst in the sky. She hated how wonderful it had been.

'Don't you want to experience that again? If not with me, then...' He cleared his throat. 'Someone else?'

Her blood quickened. That was the problem. *Never* with someone else. It was only he who made her inner siren emerge. Not that she'd admit that—he'd take too much egotistical pleasure from it. 'Relationships. Affairs,' she mumbled. 'All that stuff...it's too much effort.'

'Effort?' He shot her a startled look. 'It didn't take much effort from either of us the other night.'

Right. Again. 'That was just...'

She tightened her grip on her clutch purse. She didn't want to analyse this.

His gaze narrowed. 'You put so much effort into your work, you obviously think *that* effort is worth it.'

'Of course.'

'But you don't think what happened the other night is worth a little more *effort*?'

Sometimes the best defence was offence. 'I don't think *you're* in any real position to talk to me about making an effort.'

He laughed. 'Meaning?'

'You constantly acquire big only to then discard almost everything,' she said. 'Isn't it exhausting?'

'Are we talking about women here or—'

'Buying companies.' After all, that was his real passion. 'Breaking them up. Selling the best parts off in packages and letting the rest decay. Don't *you* ever want to put long-term *effort* into one of them? You're all about quick returns and moving on to the next project. Surely there's no real satisfaction in such fast turnover?'

'I'm very satisfied with my returns,' he said smugly. 'My talent is spotting the acquisition. Helberg is obvious—so obvious that I've got serious competition for it. Other acquisitions aren't always as clear-cut.'

'You like finding those ones best. Spotting the treasure before others see it. You like getting to them first...' She inhaled deep, pleased she was back to being annoyed with him. He was so annoyingly confident and capable. He was all cream—rising to the top in everything, all the time.

'You don't know *me*, Skylar.'

'I know plenty,' she scoffed. 'You were literally the poster boy at our old school.'

'And of course you paid close attention to some poster— to everything you were taught,' he drawled. 'Such a *good* student. You think you see everything? Perception and reality are often two very different things. Won't you consider that maybe you're misinformed?'

'Then *educate* me,' she snapped. 'Properly.'

His pupils flared.

She wanted him to *school* her. *Badly.* Being this close to him was torture. But being closer still was as effortless as breathing—was bliss. She ached for that. She stared at his mouth hovering just above hers. Seconds became centuries again and it took her too long to realise that he was speaking. It was the softest, most strained of whispers.

'I think you'd better go inside, Skylar.'

CHAPTER NINE

'YOU WANT ME to meet you where?' Zane asked haughtily but bit back a smile at the same time.

'Montague's. The jewellers on Fifth Avenue,' she said smugly. 'You know the one.'

'Yeah, I know.' He also knew she was biting back her laugh too.

She thought she could make today's Helberg reconnaissance mission his worst nightmare. But she couldn't be more wrong, because he'd been dreaming about seeing her again for days. Good, hot dreams. Which—now he stopped to consider it—were nightmares, given he was only supposed to look at and not touch the very precious treasure that was Skylar Bennet. Oh, but she was the perfect jewel with which to decorate his bed. That he'd been warned off all those years ago only made him want her more now she'd crossed his path again. Her father wasn't there to protect her now. And she didn't need him. She could protect herself. She wasn't silent with him. Wasn't well behaved. She was spirited and sarcastic as hell and he relished it so much he couldn't resist provoking her more. Because she couldn't seem to stop herself reacting to him. Which was good. It made them even.

'Ever been inside?' she followed up too innocently.

'You know I haven't.'

'Actually, I wouldn't have picked that,' she countered breezily. 'Don't you buy sparkling goodbye gifts for all those women you date?'

'No. I don't pay them off with trinkets and baubles.'

'You just leave them broken-hearted?'

'Empty-handed,' he corrected coolly. 'Because they don't need recompense for spending time with me.'

'Because they're just so very, very lucky already?' Her laughter was soft but he was certain the dimple was out.

'As well *you* know,' he purred. 'Why this jewellery store?' He prolonged the conversation because this date was still too many hours away and he liked hearing her voice. He'd missed it all week. Wednesday hadn't come quick enough. 'It doesn't even have the Helberg name.'

'Because it's only still in existence *because* of Helberg. Because they bought it into the family.'

'You think Helberg is a family?' His smile faded. 'Skylar, you know you don't have to repay the chance Reed gave you with your absolute soul—'

'And I'm not. It isn't just about the scholarship. And yes, Helberg Holdings is family. It's nice to feel needed there and valued for the things I do.'

'You ought to feel needed and valued *regardless* of what you do,' he growled. 'You ought to be needed and valued just for being you.'

There was a moment of silence down the phone.

'Did you get hit on the head?' she asked.

He'd taken a hit of some kind, apparently. But he laughed, relieved that she'd gone for a joke because he really didn't know where that had come from either. He'd go to her damned jewellery store and now he understood her motivation it made sense that her modus operandi regarding Helberg was the human connection. She wanted him to meet more of *her* work family. She didn't want him to break them up.

'Who are you going to fob me off onto this time?' he muttered, still unable to end the call.

'The jeweller.'

'Thrilling. Anyone else?'

'The sales manager. They're both lovely. They both have a lot to share.'

'Can't wait.' The sad fact was that wasn't even a lie.

Montague's was the high-end manufacturing jewellery arm of the business that Adam Courtenay was most interested in. No surprise there, given jewels were already Adam's family deal. But this was a flagship store—all exquisite space, gleaming luxury and not a price tag in sight. Zane grimaced as he looked around the plush premises three hours after he'd hung up on Skylar.

'Is the sight of all the engagement rings giving you hives?' She stole up beside him and chuckled.

Glancing down, he saw the amusement dancing in her eyes. Her dimple appeared the second he smiled back at her. He had to freeze and process the urge to haul her close and kiss her hello. He'd kiss her until she was breathless and begging for more. Then for mercy. Because he would tease her to the edge and back over and over again. Torment her the way she was tormenting him right now. Night after night he thought about her and what he'd do the second he had another chance.

He couldn't believe he'd squandered that opportunity. He'd been a fool. A teen all over again. So fast. Far too fast. The fire had consumed them both. And it wasn't enough. He gritted his teeth. She was a crush from his teen years. She should mean nothing now. But that old ache was back.

She'd been the only one he *couldn't* have. The only one he'd become bitter about. So maybe she was the only one who he was going to need to have more than once.

'Come on,' she said.

She was too bright-eyed. Too trusting. Guilt rose in a tsunami-like wave this time. He hadn't told her everything that had happened between him and Reed. But he hadn't exactly reneged on his deal with her—he'd told her some, just not *all* of the truth. Which wasn't cheating. Some wounds cut too deep to be exposed. But she'd guessed there had to be more. And he needed distraction from this already.

'You don't wear jewellery.' He cocked his head and teased her. 'Is such adornment too much *effort*?'

'Do *you* wear any?' She bit right back as he'd known she would.

'I like a good watch.' He shrugged.

Her eyes widened in faux awe. 'So you know when it's time to leave?'

He smiled appreciatively. This was what he needed—for her to spar with him, not stand by silently. He'd known—even all those years ago—that she'd have smart things to say. And he liked that she wasn't afraid to call him out. The wealthier he'd become, the more people said yes around him. The less they challenged or argued. They started to treat everything he said as immutable law. Which was rubbish. It was also—frankly—boring. Skylar was fresh.

'I sometimes wear rings too,' he said.

'To ward off evil spirits? Or all those women setting themselves at you?'

'For fun.' He moved closer, unable to stop himself. 'Which apparently is a foreign concept for you.' He brushed the backs of his fingers lightly against her cheekbone, then swept wider, noting the tiny holes in her earlobes. 'Let's look at the earrings.'

'Zane—'

'You have a graceful neck.' He had no qualms whatsoever about hijacking her expedition and thwarting her. 'You should wear long earrings to show it off.' He moved to the cabinet before she could attempt to argue more. He was aware of her watching as he assessed the collection. The ruby and diamond drops caught his attention immediately. Red definitely had to be her colour—as striking and sensual as she was. 'Can we have a closer look at those, please.'

The assistant couldn't move fast enough.

'Zane—'

'Beautiful, don't you think?' He was seriously enjoying himself.

She stared round-eyed at him and then finally at the glittering jewels he held towards her. 'They'll get caught in my hair,' she said dismissively.

'You wear your hair up more often than not. Try them on.'

'I can't—'

'It's no problem, I'm sure.' Zane smiled at the assistant, who hurried to nod.

He turned his focus back to Skylar. A hint of smokiness clouded her eyes. He knew she was tempted, which was *super* interesting—yeah, she was a sensualist who liked nice things. She just didn't let herself indulge very often. Why was she so damned studious—so restrained—even after all this time? Even after her father had passed? The guy had been controlling and overprotective. She'd basically been under house arrest. She'd gone to school. She'd gone for her runs in the mornings. And that was it.

Zane had been housebound because of his injuries. He'd

worked hard to get strong enough to leave. But Skylar had sat studying on her balcony for hours—silently watching the world, seemingly unbothered by her father's controls. And even after she'd left home, even after her father had died…she'd stayed as self-contained. Indeed, as the rubies gleamed prettily in the light, she didn't move. *Why?*

'We'll take them,' he said to the assistant without lifting his gaze from Skylar.

His smile widened as he saw her jaw tense. He knew her drilled-deep manners and good behaviour stopped her from arguing with him in front of the entire store. He stepped up to the counter and completed the transaction.

To his astonishment, that's when Skylar suddenly spoke up.

'Don't box them.' She smiled at the assistant. 'I'll wear them out.'

The assistant's eyes widened but she hustled. Zane was simply speechless as within less than a minute Skylar stood adorned with rubies and diamonds dangling from her ears, and he couldn't take his gaze off her gleaming eyes.

'You can buy them but the second I take them out I'm giving them back to you,' she murmured the moment the assistant left them, clearly well trained to know when to leave her customers to consider their other options.

'Sure.' He shrugged. 'No matter.'

'What are you going to do with them then? Wear them yourself? Give them to someone else?'

The edge in her voice pressed on his pleasure nerve because it sounded a little like jealousy. 'I'm going to look at them and think of you. Often.'

She shook her head. 'And why would you want to do that?'

'Well, I already think of you often—'

'Don't,' she breathed suddenly.

He stopped doing everything instantly—moving, breathing. Hell, even his heart stopped for a second.

'Don't flirt with me,' she finished so very softly. 'I'm doing what you want already—I'll be your companion in public. You don't have to...'

'Be honest?' He watched her intently.

He'd known the gift would bother her and yeah, that was partly why he'd given it to her. But he'd also wanted to see her in those earrings really badly and he just couldn't not buy them. And yeah, he liked this. Her challenging him. When she pushed. She was the only person to look at him with undisguised irritation at times.

But now she stepped back and instinctively he reached for her hand and stopped her. 'You don't ever treat yourself at the shops? Or ever let someone else treat you a little?'

Her eyes flashed. 'Dropping however many thousand you've just dropped isn't some *little* treat.'

Right. Good point. 'You're awfully serious, Skylar. You never do anything just for the heck of it?'

'You know I don't. Well, almost never.' She shot him a look. 'It's the way I was raised.'

He nodded his head slowly because he knew that was accurate. 'Your dad didn't let you wear any jewellery.'

She stiffened. 'We couldn't afford it. We needed other things—you know, like food.'

No. It wasn't only the money. It was her overprotective, controlling dad. 'He didn't let you do lots of things.'

It hung between them yet again. Zane had been too stunned—and yes, too hurt—to ever stop and deeply consider why she'd been so silent. Why she'd turned and run. He'd just felt rejected twice over. The best moment he'd ever experienced had devolved into a nightmare in less than a second. She'd not defended him—not admitted that she'd been as much to 'blame' as he. Zane had actually loitered in the grounds the day after, hoping to catch her on her run. She'd not appeared. And now—far too late—he wondered how scared she'd been of her father. Had he punished her?

Zane had never heard shouting, or seen any evidence of it. He'd thought the man had just been overprotective as hell of his beautiful daughter.

'You didn't rebel even once you left home? Didn't spoil yourself with your first proper pay?' Zane asked her now. 'Or are you still obeying the rules he set for you back then—putting his wishes ahead of your own desires.'

She stiffened. 'My father wanted the best for me and I knew how tough it was for him dealing with me on his own. But you're not entirely wrong. He was strict. Protective. He wanted me to prioritise my studies and then my career.'

'You weren't allowed out.' His anger stirred. 'You were *never* allowed to go out. You were always there.'

It rippled again. That memory.

'But your ears are pierced,' he said slowly. 'So when did he let that happen?'

'My mother took me not long before she left.'

Another memory flashed—one from far further back. When she'd been a little girl and he'd given her his last piece of candy because she'd been crying because her mother had gone.

'Dad had a fit,' she added softly. 'When she left he threw all her jewellery away.'

'She didn't take it with her?'

'She didn't take anything. She left it all.'

Including her daughter.

'He didn't think you might want it?'

'She left with another man and never looked back. I

guess he thought it was tainted. He threw away my earrings too.'

Yeah, her dad had tried to control the one thing he'd had
left. 'He wouldn't let you do anything.' He looked at her.
'No earrings. No dates. No fun.'

'Actually, most of that was really *my* choice.' She stepped
close and her brown eyes bore into him. 'At first I thought if
I were really, really good, then she might come back.' She
still spoke softly but somehow that made her rising emotion all the more audible. 'And then I started to worry that
if I wasn't really good, *he* might leave as well.'

Zane stood very still, inwardly stuffing down the pain
that had risen so sharply. He'd felt that desperate desire to
hold on to someone—to somehow make them stay. But his
dad hadn't wanted him from the start.

And Zane had been hard on his mother. Because where
Skylar had been obedient, it had taken him a while to get
on board. He'd been endlessly curious. A wandering child,
who'd made his mother's life difficult.

'So yes, I was good. I worked hard. And of course I did
what I was told.'

Including obeying her dad when he'd yelled at her for
kissing him. She'd been what, sixteen?

'That's why that scholarship was so important,' she said.
'It was an acceptable escape.'

Right. He sighed. And yet it still seemed to him that she
hadn't escaped all that much. She was still living in such
a constrained way. Like a nun.

'I don't blame you for wanting the scholarship,' he said
huskily. 'I blame Helberg for using it to control people.
To make them bow and scrape before him. It was a power
trip for him.'

Skylar tried to regain control of her emotions. She'd just

told Zane far too much that was too personal. But bow and scrape? Her interview with old man Helberg hadn't been like that. 'His foundation gave lots of people like me an out. You did it all on your own. Most of us ordinary people can't.'

She gently fingered the cool stones dangling from her ears. She'd started wearing earrings again a few years ago. Just little studs, nothing like these stunning things. But they didn't even feel that heavy. She liked the sensuality and the sparkle and the sway when she tilted her head. She liked the way Zane's gaze tracked them when she did. The way it lingered on her skin. She could almost feel it.

'But I bet your father was proud of you,' he said huskily.

Oh, yes. He had been. She'd been so studious and careful and yes, eager to please. But she'd got to Helberg HQ and not really made the moves she'd thought she would. And that wasn't because she hadn't worked hard. But her father had wanted her to stay. To keep trying. And once he'd gone, staying there seemed to matter all the more. She'd promised her father, and for him there was nothing worse than someone breaking their promise. She'd never wanted to let him down in the way her mother had.

'Skylar—'

'I didn't tell you that to make you pity me or whatever. But maybe you're right about my treat-free existence,' she breathed out. 'I've been focused on my work for a long time. So have you.'

'In many ways we're not so dissimilar.' He nodded, all serious.

But she laughed because he'd definitely had his treats along the way. 'I'm nothing like you.'

All those parties he'd gone to? They hadn't affected

his business success at all. Maybe she should have gone to some.

He tilted his head and a speculative gleam entered his eyes. 'You came to that Independence Day party to try to see me. What was your approach going to be?'

She flicked her hand carelessly, covering up her own cluelessness. 'I hadn't worked out the finer details.'

'You were willing to use a social situation to pursue a business interest.' He leaned close. 'Which means you and I are not so very different after all.'

'There's a vast difference between a tasteless bet and just hoping to bump into someone.'

'You wanted to bump into me.' His grin flashed wickedly. 'You definitely met your goal there.'

Skylar threw him a withering glance but the next second giggled. It felt good to giggle. Even better when he laughed with her.

She glanced around and realised the jewellery store staff were keeping their distance but also keeping their eyes on them. They'd been ensconced in this corner, intimately talking in low voices for a good ten minutes. Oh well—that was probably good for Zane's bet.

But she straightened. 'Right, you're here to meet the jeweller, remember? He's worked here for sixty years.'

'He's not ready for a nice relaxing retirement?' Zane winked at her.

For the next thirty minutes she watched as he chatted with the jeweller, listening to the history of the place. The joy he found in his work. The pride. The capital funding from Helberg that had enabled their expansion. The jeweller and the manager both gazed up at him, clearly delighted to meet him. It was his smile. Everyone fell for it. Even her.

But when they finally stepped out onto the summer pavement he shook his head at her. 'You brought me to one of the most successful subsidiaries. It's been in the stable only a decade and doesn't even bear the Helberg name. What was the point?'

To make him uncomfortable. Of course, that hadn't worked. He'd flipped it on her the second he'd spotted those earrings.

She was failing already—only two weeks in. And it wasn't even a surprise because deep inside she was worried he was right about Helberg Holdings. Something had to happen with it.

Zane was only indulging her in these visits and the truth was she wanted him to indulge her in another way altogether.

Educate me. Properly.

The command she'd issued the other night circled in her head. Tempting her. The ache inside sharpened—the appetite she couldn't suppress any more. She should have all the treats she'd missed out on for so long. The physical ones. All she'd done all her life was work. Learn. Study. Stay safe. Stay focused. She'd missed out on a lot of fun. And he was the perfect person to help, right? Because he'd worked too. But he'd become far more successful than she *and* he'd had a lot of fun along the way. He really knew how. Which meant he could teach her many things. And there was no way her heart would be endangered—she still didn't actually like him all that much, right? And his heart was in no danger at all given he didn't have one…

'You have the weirdest look on your face,' he said, looking down at her.

She raised her eyebrows. 'What kind of look?'

'Cunning. Like a fox. Pretty fox.'

It was the only time in her life she'd ever been called a fox. She quite liked it.

'I don't trust it,' he added.

She chuckled. 'Shocker. You don't trust anyone.'

'Fair.' He smiled. 'You don't trust me either.'

'Not entirely true, actually. I trust you to be honest with me. You've been pretty blunt thus far.'

'Hmm. That's true. As have you. Tell me what you're thinking.'

'That I'm no longer a virgin but I'm still inexperienced in bed.'

Such raw shock pinched his features that she bit back a laugh.

His fingertips touched a spot on her left cheek. 'You should always laugh when you feel the urge. Don't hold back, Skylar.'

'Well, I've still no experience in an actual bed, have I?' Heat trammelled through her and she inadvertently swayed towards him before catching herself and straightening.

'And that's what you want? More experience. In bed. With me.'

'Right,' she breathed huskily. 'You're skilled.'

'I can't decide if I'm honoured or offended.'

'You're honoured. We both know that. We also both know you're going to agree.' And she was crossing both fingers behind her back and hoping like crazy she was right.

'I am?'

'You can't resist a game.'

'Is that what this is?'

'You can consider it a challenge if you like.' Her temperature soared but she pushed on lightly. 'For me this is a learning journey.'

'A learning journey?' He started to laugh. 'Wow, that's

so HR of you. Will you want to set some goals? Get a performance appraisal afterwards?'

'That's really not a bad idea—'

'Flow chart? Bonus points for creativity?'

'For all sorts of things.' She nodded.

'No.' He shook his head. 'No, no, no.'

She died inside. 'You're declining my offer?'

'I'm declining the flow chart and bullet points.' He stepped right into her space and put his hand gently on her shoulder. 'This can't be business between us. This is play.'

'Surely you like a game to have rules?' She instinctively knew she needed them.

'Don't you realise how much I hate rules?'

'There have to be *some* boundaries.' For safety—to protect her heart, right?

'Tell me something.' He ran his thumb gently back and forth across her lower lip in the softest, most sensual of touches. 'Why are you suddenly willing to make the effort?'

Her legs barely held her up as relief then arousal slammed into her. 'There's not much effort required for this.' The truth just spilled from her.

His eyebrows shot up. 'Why, Skylar, how you flatter me.'

She closed her eyes briefly and summoned the shell of strength she was going to need. 'There's no effort because this isn't a *relationship*. It's an *arrangement*.' She opened her eyes and gazed right into his. 'And to be frank, it's all about me.'

His lips twitched. 'What you want. And I get nothing?'

'You need for nothing, you've already made that clear,' she pointed out with a tiny shrug. 'But you enjoy a release every now and then and right now you can't because of that bet.'

'Every now and then...'

'Do you always repeat what people say to you?'

'Only when it's weird.'

Crushed, she flinched.

He put his other hand on her other shoulder, holding her firmly in place. 'No. Don't back out now. Tell me how you want this to work.'

He'd inched closer, and when he was closer, everything was easier.

'It's very straightforward,' she muttered. 'On your public date nights, we sleep together before I go home.'

His fingers tightened fractionally. 'So you're revising our original agreement.'

'You revise deals all the time. It's a normal part of business.'

'Right.' He huffed a breath. 'Well, revision works both ways. You want an amendment, then I get one too.'

She hesitated and looked at him warily. 'What amendment do you want?'

'You've sprung this on me. I need a little time to figure it out. I'll let you know.'

She shook her head. He was quick, he could come up with something here and now. 'I can't agree if I don't know the details.'

'You're going to *have* to trust me—more than just being honest.' He suddenly smiled. 'That's the real challenge, isn't it.'

'As if it isn't for you?'

Ignoring the passers-by on the street, he stepped in even closer and lowered his head towards hers. The intimacy seared—it might as well only be the two of them in the world. She was certain he was about to kiss her—indeed, as he spoke, his lips almost, almost brushed hers.

'You want your learning journey, Skylar? All you have to do is say yes.'

CHAPTER TEN

SKYLAR STRUGGLED TO BREATHE. Her pretty rented dress was short. She had only a thin slip beneath it and a tiny scrap of silk beneath that. But she was still too hot and she couldn't release enough of her nervous energy either. She'd said yes, of course, but this wasn't the straight-to-bed evening she'd secretly been aching for. He'd brought her to dinner at one of those restaurants that you needed to book a year in advance. Unless you were a young billionaire with half the internet following your every move. Then you could just walk in and be given the best table. And waste a whole lot of time. All she wanted was to be alone with him. In bed. Now that she'd said yes, Skylar was appallingly impatient.

'You want to share some mini plates?' he muttered.

She nodded. 'You pick.'

She watched him study the menu. It took an age—and all she did was note how his dark shirt and trousers emphasised his handsome features. He was stunningly good-looking. But it was the gleam in his eyes and the twitch at the corner of his mouth that got her the most.

He was good-humoured. And a tease.

Eventually the dishes he'd selected arrived—plate after plate of small snacks. So many plates. She nibbled to be polite. To pass the too slowly ticking time. To her surprise, he picked as little as she did, before he suddenly pushed his plate away and vehemently sighed. She arched her eyebrows at him.

'I'm not hungry,' he growled in answer.

'Then why did you order all this food?' She gestured at the laden table.

He rolled his shoulders. 'I was trying to distract myself.'

'From…?'

He shot her a sizzling look.

'We didn't need to come out to dinner,' she said quietly.

He released another massive sigh. 'Yes, we did.'

She'd forgotten about the public aspect to their dates. 'Well, now what?' she asked, seeing as dinner was done for them both. 'Should we go to a club?'

'No.'

'You don't want to go dancing?'

'I really want to dance with you,' he ground out. 'Just not in public.'

'Aren't we supposed to be seen in public? Aren't we here right now for the photos that waiter is surreptitiously taking?'

'No,' he contradicted her shortly. 'We're here to slow down.'

'To…*what*?'

He shot her another of those smouldering looks. 'You know once we start, we're like a runaway train. So out of control.'

'Yes,' she breathed. *Exactly*. That was the bit she liked best, actually.

'So we need to slow down,' he muttered.

'Why—'

'Because you deserve more than a quick—'

'I like quick,' she interrupted.

He closed his eyes. 'Not helping, Skylar.'

Good. 'Haven't I waited long enough?'

He gazed at her fiercely—a picture of hungry, virile man. 'All the more reason to slow down and do this properly.'

She really didn't want this whole slow approach. 'I said yes, you don't need to woo me with dinner.'

He paused. 'Maybe I'm ensuring you have adequate fuel on board.'

'I already have more energy than I know what to do with,' she said. 'I can hardly sit still.'

'*Damn it*, Skylar.' But his smile suddenly flashed.

She couldn't resist provoking him a little more. 'You just don't believe in boring Saturday nights at home.'

He gaped at her for a moment. 'This one isn't going to be boring.'

He stood up, tossed a sheaf of cash on the table and jerked his head towards the exit. 'If you don't want more of a scene, move now.'

Skylar grabbed her purse and half skipped to keep up with him. Delighted.

But then the chauffeur didn't drive fast enough for her. She was aware of Zane watching her, that half smile on his face, but keeping his damned distance the entire ride.

Finally they turned into the basement parking lots of one of the needle-thin, super-tall, billionaire tower blocks on the southern edge of Central Park. The chauffeur held the door for them then Zane led her to the elevator and punched several numbers on the keypad. Moments later, they stepped into the elevator. Unable to resist, she looked up at him, met his wild gaze.

But he shook his head. 'No. Not yet.'

They whizzed skywards in the smooth, silent lift. The

second the doors opened, Zane stepped forward. For a split second she watched him—a tall silhouette against floor-to-ceiling windows. Her pulse trebled its tempo. She drew a steadying breath and followed.

'Your apartment is incredible,' she said. It was like a palace in the sky. The city and Central Park stretched below them for miles. 'The view is amazing. So is the one from your Belhaven beach house.'

'Yeah,' he said. 'I've been to beautiful beaches all around the world—the Mediterranean, the Caribbean, Hawaii, off the coast of Australia, but none of them beat that one.'

'Because it's home.' She zipped and unzipped her little purse, desperately burning just a smidge of the energy that had been firing around her body for days. 'I've never been to any other beaches. Never been overseas. Not even out of state.'

'Not ever?'

'No.' She paced, taking in other details with hyper-awareness. There was a vast computer screen set-up in the place others might have as a dining area. There was a stunning open plan kitchen. Intricately woven rugs on the beautiful wooden flooring. Glancing back, she saw he'd not moved from the window. He was as still as before, still just staring at her.

'What's wrong with you?' she teased. 'Are you glued to the floor?'

'Apparently.'

The strain in his voice emboldened her and she walked back to where he stood. 'What should I do?'

He released a deep sigh and shook his head again. 'I'm not going to teach you how to please me.'

She paused. She'd kind of thought that was the point.

'You need to learn to please yourself.' He reached into

his pocket and pulled out a foil strip of condoms and held them out to her. 'Do what you want. How you want. You need to figure out what you want and what you like.'

She still didn't quite understand.

'Tonight you're taking the lead,' he added with a mocking grin.

And that was not what she wanted. At all. She just wanted him to sweep her back into that fiery caldron—to seduce her. Completely. She had no idea how or where to begin.

He watched her for another moment and that smile softened. 'Okay, look, given your inexperience, I'm gonna assume you've never seen a naked man before. Shall I strip for you?'

'Well.' She took the protection and gripped it ridiculously tightly. 'You did say you wanted to dance.'

'You want me to put some music on?'

'No,' she snapped. 'No more time wasting. Strip. Do it now.'

He chuckled delightedly but began unbuttoning his shirt. Slowly. One button after another, captivating her as his skin was revealed. His chest was gorgeous—broad, muscled, a smattering of hair that trailed down…

Her fingertips tingled. He tossed the shirt to the floor, then his hands went to his belt.

'Look. Touch. Don't touch,' he muttered, holding her gaze as he worked the buckle. Then the button. The zipper. 'Dance with me. Whatever you want. However fast. However slow. Your choice.' He shoved down his trousers and stepped out of them.

She drew in a sharp breath.

'You know I was in a car accident,' he said ruefully. 'It was probably on that stupid poster about me at school.'

It hadn't been on the poster, but she knew—though not any personal details. She'd never seen scars like this. His thigh was like patchwork. 'You studied from home while you recovered.'

'Rehab took a long time. There are a few metal pins. I set off airport security alarms—'

He set off every alarm—*warning, dangerously charming man ahead*. 'So basically you're bionic now.'

'It doesn't hinder my performance if that's what you're worried about.'

'I'm not worried.' She stepped closer. 'But I don't think I want a *performance*.'

'Right.' He shoved down his boxers.

Skylar stared. Super-hot and super…stunned. Just stunned.

'Skylar?'

'Mmmm?'

'Did you run this morning?' he asked, slowly walking towards her.

'Of course,' she answered on auto. 'I haven't missed a Saturday-morning run in more than two years.'

'Impressive.'

Yeah, that wasn't what was impressive here. He was completely, beautifully naked.

'It makes you feel good?'

'Yes,' she mumbled. She couldn't take her eyes off his body—his smooth olive skin, the sleek muscles, the rippling abs, the slim hips, the…

'Why don't we find out what else makes you feel good.'

'Okay.' She paused. 'You're really…'

'Turned on?'

He was. He very much was. And she was *so* hot. 'It's been a full two weeks since we… That's not what you're used to. Of course you must be feeling frustrated,' she muttered.

'It's you I want to feel.'

She shook her head. He was a virile man, that was all.

He huffed a little laugh. 'How can you not believe me?' He drew in a deep breath. 'Seeing is believing. *Feeling* for yourself might be even better.'

Oh. 'You want me to—'

'Do whatever you want with me,' he said with exaggerated patience. 'Any time you like. I'm clearly *ready* for whatever, whenever you are.'

He certainly was. Skylar inhaled another deep breath and released it slowly, determined to get a hold of herself. This was an *opportunity* and she was going to make the most of it.

'You're saying I can do anything?' she asked innocently, lifting her chin. 'You want a safe word?'

His jaw dropped.

'*Stop* should suffice, don't you think?' she added.

He just stayed there staring at her. She smiled happily. She'd rendered him speechless. There was a first. Confidence trickled into her veins. There was no denying he was hot for her. Which was really, really good.

'Do you think you could sit down?' she muttered. 'You're too tall for me to—'

'Chair? Sofa? Bed?'

Bed was too far away. 'Sofa.'

He took position in the centre of the large sofa and looked up at her as she stood in front of him, his cheeks slightly flushed. She'd spent so long watching for him— *waiting*—and now he was before her, naked. Willing to do whatever she wanted. She really didn't know where to start.

But then…then, she did. She knew what she wanted. She stepped forward and straddled him, a knee either side of his thighs. Right on his lap. His lips parted but he said nothing. She smiled and put the packet of protection beside them. It was time to touch. Just the lightest brush of her fingertips down his chest. Goose bumps lifted on his skin. His nipples tightened. Unable to resist the urge, she leaned forward and licked one.

'Okay, Skylar.' He stretched his arms wide along the back of the sofa and gripped the leather in his fists. 'Okay.' His breathing shortened. 'This is your game, sweetheart... you take the lead. I'm not...not going to interfere.'

She smiled, unsure if he was telling her that again or reminding himself of his mission. And frankly, she still *wanted* him to interfere. So maybe she was going to have to make him. She glided her hands further over his hot, fit body. Couldn't resist leaning closer, breathing in his heat and scent, trailing her fingertips up the side of his neck to his jaw.

'You smell nice,' she murmured. 'And you've shaved.'

'Yeah,' he muttered. 'Thought I ought to in case you wanted me to kiss you in some...uh...sensitive areas.'

She stared into his eyes, her brain shorting at the image he'd just put in her head. 'I appreciate your consideration.'

He swallowed. Hard. 'I was happy to make the effort for you.'

Oh. He was tricky. She slid her hand back down his chest and felt the thump of his heart. It was fast and his skin was more than warm to the touch now—a sheen of sweat glistened on him. She slid her hand lower. 'Are you okay?'

'Actually, I'm not sure my lungs are working properly,' he muttered. 'It's getting quite hard to breathe.'

Pleasure and power surged. Even if it were only right now and only physical, he *wanted* her. A lot. 'You might need a little mouth-to-mouth?'

'You think it might help?' His smile lifted.

She chuckled too, a different kind of warmth adding to her molten temperature. She pressed her mouth gently to his. It rushed back on her—this silken, sudden delight, and she remembered the total pleasure of tangling like this with him. The heat they generated together.

Detonation all over again. Suddenly there was no restraint within her. Her touch firmed, teasing, testing—getting to know the indentations of his body—the firm muscle stretched over long bones. Then she swept lower, seeking out his most sensitive areas—stroking, teasing, *tasting*.

'You've done some research, Skylar?' he growled, his hips lifting beneath her ministrations.

She flushed and glanced up at him because yeah, she had. 'I might've read a few articles in the last couple of days.'

He groaned and his head fell back against the sofa. 'I… uh…appreciate your studious preparation.'

She almost purred under his praise but in moments was lost in her exploration of him. He was beautiful, and the freedom to discover every inch of him was too delicious.

'I like it when you play with me. Skylar—' He broke off on another groan.

She moved faster, stroking him with two hands and then taking him deep into her mouth…ever so slowly.

'Jeez, Skylar.' He tensed beneath her.

Yeah. This was *hot*.

'Two more strokes,' he growled, suddenly impatient. 'Two more…'

She gave him one. And then stalled, lifting her face to watch his reaction. His eyes flashed open and he gazed down at her. His pupils were blown, his cheeks flushed.

'Oh.' His breath hissed but he smiled like a feral wolf. 'Is that how it is?'

'Yeah,' she breathed. 'That's how it is.'

She wanted to torture him—the very best kind of torture.

He closed his eyes, the strained agony of being this close to ecstasy made him so damned handsome. 'You realise you'll get it back three-fold.'

'Fantastic.' The only problem was that she was close too. So hot. So close. And she wanted to come. She ran her hands along his arms, still stretched wide along the sofa, and gripped his wrists and tried to tug them. 'I need you.'

'Need me to what?' he baited, resisting her attempts to make him move.

'You know,' she breathed. 'Please.'

'Touch you? Kiss you?'

'Do *everything* to me,' she muttered.

He moved, gripping her waist to take him with her as he simply slid from the sofa to the floor. She toppled to the side, easing off his lap to roll onto her back.

She gazed up at him, feeling hedonistic and hot. 'Kiss every inch of me,' she muttered, finally getting the hang of making her wishes known. 'Every inch.'

His smile was utterly wolfish. 'My appetite has returned and I'm ravenous, Skylar. So I might do more than kiss.'

'Sounds good.'

He lavished her with licks and nips, touches. Her nipples ached, tight and needy, while deep in her core she melted. She reached for him and he pushed her with his big hands, sliding them down her body to hold her squirming thighs apart. He kissed the tops of her inner thighs, kissed her more intimately than that. She closed her eyes, loving the sensations he gave her. 'More.'

He paused. She whimpered. She didn't want him to tease her now. She just wanted him. *'Zane...'*

He must've heard her plea because he filled her with his fingers and sucked right where she was so sensitive.

She came. Hard. But even as she moaned helplessly, she asked again and arched, utterly open before him. 'More. I want you *with* me.'

He took only a moment to prepare and then was back. 'Skylar.'

She curled her arm around his neck to keep him close to her, looking into his beautiful eyes. He pressed close. Yes. This was what she wanted. What she'd always want. Zane with her. His body moving within hers. She wrapped her leg around his hip and got grabby, gasping as she worked to get closer to him still. His hands firmed, holding her so he could grind.

'You want me as deep as it gets?' he growled.

'Yes. Deep.' She shuddered. 'Really deep.'

He worked harder, pushing into a rhythm that was fierce and fast and everything. She shook, her eyes closing as her tension burst and a white-hot orgasm hit. This was it. This was the best feeling of her whole damned life.

When she could finally open her eyes again, she found him holding her, watching her, still breathing hard.

'That was…' He shook his head almost helplessly.

'Awesome. Just awesome.' She would never move again.

'Yeah.' Zane released her slowly and rose to his feet. 'Back in a sec.'

It was no time before he was back. He bent and handed her a glass. She sipped without querying the contents, then spluttered on a laugh.

'Is this electrolytes?' She held the glass up to the light. *'Seriously?'*

'You need them. I sure do. And if our recovery is fast, then we can carry on. So drink up.'

She was very glad to know they would be carrying on. So she drained the glass.

He inclined his head and chuckled. 'Full marks, sweetheart. You really are stellar.'

'Full marks to you too.' She laughed as his eyebrows lifted. 'What, you don't think you should get graded because you're the more experienced one?' She batted her lashes at him. 'Have you not heard of three-sixty assessments?'

'I'll give you three-sixty.'

She yelped and giggled as he pulled her back against him and she felt his laughter rumble in his chest.

Getting him to upskill her education was best idea she'd ever had.

'I should get going,' she mumbled a couple of hours later.

'You what?' Zane questioned with full authority. 'Class isn't over, Skylar. I thought you were a diligent student. The sort who puts in *lots* of extra hours. The kind who pulls all-nighters in fact.' He rolled out of his massive bed and threw her a T-shirt. 'You just need more sustenance.'

'Not more electrolytes,' she moaned.

'Definitely something a little more substantial.'

She didn't argue with him. She didn't want to leave. After the electrolytes, he'd carried her to his shower. Helped her bathe—thoroughly—then carried her to his bed. She quite appreciated all the carrying. She appreciated the attentions in his bed even more.

Now she followed him to the kitchen, and while he pulled things from the cupboards, she sneaked peeks at the shelves. 'You use all these fancy ingredients?'

'I have a chef on call. He's here most afternoons to make my dinner and prep breakfast and lunch that I just have to assemble. But I can cook for myself when I need to.'

'And what do you cook?' She watched as he took a pan from a drawer and got a stick of butter from the fridge.

'Protein pancakes.'

'Protein?' She giggled.

'I had them for dinner almost every night. I still love them.' He got busy with a couple bowls, eggs, flour and a whisk.

Skylar got busy watching.

'When you're in recovery, you need the best nutrition you can get,' he lectured her with a laugh.

He had been in recovery for a while with that leg injury.

'Four operations,' he said. 'I know you're wondering.'

These weren't box pancakes. These were made from scratch and were thick, fluffy and enormous.

'These are really good.'

'Why are you so surprised?' he asked with mild outrage. 'I told you I made them all the time when I was growing up.'

'Your mother's recipe?'

'No.' He glanced at the fridge. 'She worked late.'

'So you made them for her too?' She just knew he had. 'They're so good.'

'I have a far wider assortment of toppings now.' He placed a pack of strawberries on the counter. Then a bottle of maple syrup. A can of whipped cream. A bottle of caramel sauce, another of chocolate. He looked at the array and then looked at her with that wicked gleam in his eyes. 'What do you think? You like any of these?'

His playfulness stoked her own. 'I like all of them.'

His smile widened. 'You have an adventurous appetite, Skylar?'

'It seems that I do.' She ran her fingers down the cool can of cream and shot him a wicked smile. 'Adventurous *and* voracious.'

* * *

Zane watched her sleep. Yeah, it was weird of him to do it but he really didn't want to wake her. He was too busy feeling smug. She was in such a deep sleep. He'd not just satisfied her—repeatedly—he'd exhausted her. And she'd exhausted him. This morning, he'd woken the latest he had in *years*. Yet he wasn't entirely satisfied. He wanted to see her indulge in more—of all the sorts of thing she'd decided were too much 'effort.' Having fun. Treating herself. Holidays. Finding a new job even?

Because it struck him that she'd stalled. And it bothered him. Even though it shouldn't. It was her life, not any business of his to interfere in. But they could have some more fun together. They could do that right now. Well, as soon as she woke.

And when she finally stirred, he didn't give her time to feel awkward. He'd keep this as effortless as possible.

'Come on. Let's go to the local market and get brunch,' he ordered.

'Brunch?' Her eyes gleamed but then immediately dimmed. 'I can't wear that dress at this time of day.'

'I've got something you—'

'I'm not wearing your sweatpants again.'

He chuckled. Yeah. 'Not those.' He handed her the bag he'd retrieved from the lift.

She pulled out the jeans, the tee, and shot him quite the stunned look. 'When did you get these?'

'They were delivered a few minutes ago.' Because he'd predicted the problem. 'Want to shower before getting dressed?'

That look turned sultry. 'Want to join me?'

'Absolutely.'

It was another hour before they were dressed and headed towards the elevator.

'I guess this way you can get morning-after photos,' she said thoughtfully.

Zane hesitated, his finger hovering above the button to summon the elevator. That hadn't occurred to him and certainly hadn't been the reason he'd suggested they go out. 'Does that bother you? We can always order in if you'd rather.'

'I don't mind the photos or the speculation.' She shrugged airily. '*Not* caring what others think is the other thing I'm learning from you.'

CHAPTER ELEVEN

SKYLAR TOSSED AND TURNED. It was well after midnight and she couldn't sleep a wink. She'd finally be seeing Zane again tomorrow—taking him on their next Helberg visit. Though secretly she wished it was Saturday tomorrow. Another date night. Last Saturday should have been enough. It wasn't. Even though it had bled into Sunday. She was losing sight of her goal, prioritising the pleasure he could give her instead. Maybe her father was right—lust led you from the path and into selfishness. All the more reason to sate that lust, then, right? Because it would ease eventually, surely.

Her phone rang. She glanced at the caller ID and answered before thinking better of it.

'It's me.'

'Yeah.' She was glad he couldn't see the smile on her face. 'What do you want?'

'I was thinking about you.'

'So you decided to phone and wake me up?'

'You weren't asleep anyway. You answered too quickly and you sound wide-awake and breathless. Why are you breathless?'

She gritted her teeth to stop herself laughing. 'What were you thinking about me?'

'Everything and then some.'

She could hear *his* smile. 'Oh?'

'I've been thinking about some things we didn't cover the other night.'

'Oh?' she squeaked.

'I've bet you've never had phone sex either, huh,' he purred.

'Um—'

'Think about where you'd want me to touch you if I were there now,' he said softly.

She'd spent every night this week thinking about that. Which was why she was wide-awake now.

'Skylar?'

'Mmm-hmm?'

'Touch there,' he muttered.

Her toes curled. 'Zane…'

'I dare you.'

Heat burned through her because he hadn't needed to dare, she already was. 'What about you?'

'I'm already there. I've got myself in hand and every time you sigh, I stroke.'

'Oh…'

'Yeah…like that.'

'Ohh…' She dragged in a breath. 'Faster?'

'If you want—'

She wanted. So much. 'Tell me more,' she breathed.

He muttered. Low. Hot. Dirty.

'Ohh… I… *Zane*…' As she dragged in a deep breath of recovery, she heard his groan. She flushed with pleasure again.

'Want to hear some of my other ideas?' he drawled.

'I think you should write them down,' she whispered, broken yet burning all over again.

'Bullet points?'

'Yeah. Works for me.'

His laughter was low. 'See you tomorrow, Skylar. Sweet dreams.'

Her dreams were anything but sweet.

'We're going to one of the distribution warehouses in New Jersey.' She couldn't quite look him in the eye after that phone call last night. And she knew he knew it. He looked so amused. So smug.

'Let's go in my car,' he said. 'It's a long drive.'

'Yes,' she said primly. 'How ever will we fill the time?'

She shouldn't have been so transparent. Definitely shouldn't have blurred the boundaries between their meetings about the business and their dates. But it was too late. She watched him press the button to close the privacy screen the second they were both belted in the back of the car. Then he turned, leaning above her, retribution glinting in his eyes. 'You're a temptress, Skylar Bennet.'

She stared at him.

'You drive me crazy,' he muttered. 'Make me forget everything but what I want to do with you.'

That was the only balm on the burn searing through her—that he felt this intense drive to touch her every bit as much as she ached for it. 'And what's that?'

He kept her pinned in his gaze. She waited. His hand slid up her thigh and under the hem of her skirt. He wasn't even touching her skin to skin—hadn't slid those tormenting fingers beneath her panties. But the slow circles, the skating tips of his fingers were enough to pull her into the furnace… He wove the fingers of his other hand into her braid and kept her head tilted towards him. The smallest sinful smile curved his lips. She knew what he wanted. To watch her—this close—as he made her lose control with the gentlest, lightest of touches. Such torment. Because she knew his strength and she wanted all of him—full power. Her breathing shortened, she spread her legs, she tilted her chin. She wanted his kiss. She wanted him to lose control too, wanted him *with* her in this.

'Let go, beautiful. I'm here. I've got you,' he breathed. His blue eyes gleamed—provocative, possessive, protective. Giving her almost everything she wanted.

She sank, shuddering under the waves of bliss as they washed through her. Breathing out deeply, she looked back up into his eyes—saw the glint of satisfaction in his eyes, the strain of desire in the firm hold of his mouth.

She wanted more. Of course she wanted more. She could never concentrate now. Not on anything else until she'd made him feel the same.

The flicker of amusement in his face told her he knew. 'One, nil,' he smugly muttered.

'You're keeping a tally?' She rolled her eyes. 'Of course you're keeping a tally.'

This was all a game to him. It could be to her too, couldn't it? But with no rules at all now. The man did not play fair and there was nothing she couldn't try with him.

'What can I say, I like numbers.' He shrugged. 'You like them too. You know we have so much more in common than just our hometown. You're as competitive as I am. As focused. As driven.'

'You think?' She liked that he saw her as an equal. As a worthy competitor. She leaned across him.

He stiffened. 'What are you doing?'

She leaned a little lower. 'Evening the score.'

It took Zane for ever to realise that the car had stopped. Good thing the rear windows were tinted. Her 'evening the score' had felled him. He'd hauled her close to finally kiss her. Once he'd started, he couldn't stop. He'd kept kissing her and it had culminated in this—the complete loss of time, control, composure. Her crisp—so very HR—blouse was untucked and creased, most of the buttons undone. Her skin was flushed, her lips puffy. Her eyes were huge. Dishevelled and dazed, there was no hiding what she'd been doing. While he was just hot. So hot. And not just his shirt but his trousers were undone. He had the horrifying thought that his hunger for her was never going to end.

He pulled back from her and coughed. 'I don't think either of us are in any state to meet people.'

'No,' she agreed. 'We're just here to see property anyway. It's a site expansion.'

Zane ran his hand through his hair and tried to summon a speck of concentration. Property was Cade's interest. Whether this was the piece the guy was after, he didn't know.

'Why a blank site?' He glanced out the window. 'There's nothing here, Skylar. What are we doing?'

'It was metaphorical. I was hoping you can see the potential.'

He hated that this deal was between them. He wanted to forget about it so he could focus on seeing out this fling. Educating her in so many other ways.

'You can't, can you?' she said quietly. 'Because you're so stuck on the fact that the old boss didn't give you a scholarship? Hell, Zane. It wasn't like you needed it. You'd achieved more by the time you were twenty than he personally had.'

He could tell her the rest of his history with Reed. How truly life-changing his meeting with the man had been. How devastating. Maybe then she would understand. But he'd never told anyone all of that. Never discussed it even with his mother. And she'd been there. He didn't think he physically could. You kept your pain to yourself. You didn't complain.

'You really can't forgive and forget?' She waved at the bare plot. 'It could be a blank state. Start afresh. Rebuild it. You could do that. You could do anything.'

No, he couldn't. Not with this. 'It's going to happen anyway, Skylar. If not me then it'll be some other entity.'

Skylar was failing on several levels. To convince him. And to keep this 'arrangement' from sliding into something that meant more to her.

Maybe he was right about Helberg but she'd worked her whole life to get to where she was—and if she wasn't here, then…where? She'd been on this one path her whole life. Not daring to deviate from the plan put in place by her father so long ago. She didn't know what she was going to do going forward if it all ended—and she didn't like that uncertainty.

'You get out of HQ and come to empty plots of land quite often?' he asked her.

'I like getting about to see people on other sites. It makes me feel more connected to everyone within the company.'

'Because it's lonely in your office going from project to project?'

'I like people.'

'Yeah, I know all about how you help everyone, Bernie told me.'

'You don't think I should care about people, only profit?'

'Without profit, those people you like don't have jobs,' he said. 'That's the rapidly approaching possibility for half of Helberg's employees. Sure, some divisions are doing well, but some definitely aren't. Study the numbers, Sky-lar. I know you can see this.'

As much as she didn't want to admit it, parts were bloated and ineffectual. Divisions could be run better. Hell, she knew that better than anyone. She'd seen the senior management and their time wasting.

'Decent management might be able to turn it around,' she said obstinately.

'You don't think Reed Helberg was decent?'

'Do you really have no respect for him at all? He built a massive company. He did good in the community.'

'He *inherited* a successful company and proceeded to run it into the ground by focusing on expansion into luxury brands with little relevance to core business. He did limited charitable acts to buy praise and goodwill. To be seen as someone outstanding. But he was a selfish egotist. You know he was hardly in the office in recent years.'

She didn't want to admit that Zane might be right on that either. She'd hardly seen Reed in the office. She'd heard that in the last months he cantankerously called in with instructions and commands that sent shivers through the finance department.

'It's still worth having someone come in and try.' She drew in a breath. 'People have invested more than their time in Helberg. They've invested their money.' She tried to make him understand. 'The old employees share scheme encouraged them to invest—it was considered a sign of loyalty.'

He stilled. 'Did you invest?'

She shook her head. 'That scheme was closed to new employees a few years ago. But some of the long-timers did. Now the share price has dropped and those loans aren't repaid and...'

He inhaled deeply, cursed beneath his breath. 'Bernie?'

She nodded.

'Skylar,' he said quietly. 'Isn't that all the more reason to let someone come in and liquidate where necessary and lift the price of assets to the best possible?'

'People will lose their jobs.'

'People are made redundant every day. We'll do our best but the alternative is that it goes under completely and everyone loses their jobs.' He looked at her. 'You can't guarantee security, Skylar.'

Yeah. She knew that. She just didn't want to. And she still wished someone would try.

Zane drew a deep breath into his lungs, trying not to get distracted by her beauty again. But she came alive when she talked about her colleagues. She cared about those people passionately—her work family. And right now she made such a different picture to the wide-eyed girl he remembered silently watching the world from the top floor. The girl who'd all but crawled inside his shirt when he'd stolen a kiss from her.

He wanted another kiss now.

He liked to ensure his lovers were satisfied but his desire to satisfy *her* was on another level. He didn't just want her satisfied. He wanted her total surrender. He wanted her eyes glowing and her skin flushed and her as out of control as ever. With him. It was insane. Was it really just that interrupted kiss? That they'd not burned out their chemistry at the time, and her father's rejection had ignited another determination within him? Did he want Skylar this much because he'd been told in no uncertain terms that he couldn't have her?

But now he could. Was. Would some more. So he would get over it, right?

Because he had no intention of ever settling down. Of ever hurting a child the way he had been. Because he'd have no kids. Ever. No commitment.

He just needed to rid himself of this fixation on her. And he was sick of meeting her in offices or shops or seeing factory floors. Maybe he'd show her how spectacularly the division of assets could work in a company's favour.

'I've thought of my amendment to our arrangement,' he said huskily.

Her eyes widened.

'I don't want a date this Saturday.'

Her jaw dropped pleasingly.

'I want a whole weekend,' he added quickly. 'A long weekend. Away.'

'Where?'

'It's a surprise. But there's relevance to our business as well.'

He almost had her. Then he saw the shadows flitter in. 'I can't take time off work—'

'You worked on the last long weekend. I bet you have far too many holidays accrued. We'll fly out Friday morning, fly back Monday night.'

He'd known she'd worry about work.

They'd have whole days and nights together. He would have his fill of her. He would get control of his own mind again. Dial it back for the duration of the time they'd be dating. Because this was only a game. That was all. And this weekend would be just the thing to get it back under control.

'Would it be public?'

'No.'

'That means several days with nothing on that website.'

'No problem. We've given them enough for now.'

She shook her head. 'I can't make those arrangements that quickly. I can't just abandon all my projects. I've got too much work to do.'

He understood and respected that even though his body rebelled. 'Then we'll have a quiet weekend this weekend so you can get ahead and clear the decks. We'll go the weekend after.'

She looked tempted. But also strangely wary. 'So we won't have a date this Saturday?'

'Are you worried you're missing out?' He felt a ridiculous warmth bloom in his chest.

'No, it would be convenient, actually. I'm just concerned about your ability to have a boring night at home all alone.'

'I guess I can manage it just this once.'

CHAPTER TWELVE

SHE WASN'T MISSING HIM. Nope. And she certainly was *not* feeling disappointed there was no date tonight. She was in a good space. She'd had a good week. Great, actually. She'd been working round the clock, getting reports written. Achieving with a capital *A*. She was still working even now. Some might call it a boring Saturday night at home but she was satisfied…

Yeah, right. Of course she wasn't. She was edgy. It took everything to keep herself on track and not check her phone every five minutes in case he'd messaged.

There'd been eight messages this week—for the record. Silly comments that made her smile. A stupid meme. A copy of the latest photo of them together, which, to her shame, she'd saved as her wallpaper. And yes, she knew this arrangement wasn't a relationship, but she couldn't help herself. She was staring at it when she realised someone was pushing her buzzer. And not releasing it.

'Let me in,' he growled the second she hit the intercom.

The big bad wolf himself. She listened to his rapid thudding feet as he ran up the stairs and inwardly marvelled at his fitness given the mauling his leg must have had to be so scored with surgical scars.

'I thought you didn't want a date this week.' But she held the door open for him.

And he held a bag that smelt delicious.

'Thai.' He put it on her table. 'I was betting you hadn't had dinner.'

She recognised the sticker on the brown bag. He'd found her favourite. Her mouth watered. Then she looked at him and her mouth watered more. There was stubble on his jaw, slight shadows beneath his eyes.

'You look tired,' she said softly. He looked fit for bed.

'I've been burning the candle to get some work done. Had to travel a bit.' He frowned. 'While you look fresh as a daisy.'

She didn't feel like a daisy. She felt like a firecracker— filled with wild, endless energy that couldn't get release without ignition. But the spark had arrived and that familiar fizzing inside had begun.

'Have you got your work done?' He opened the bags and lifted out a couple of containers.

'Pretty much.' She grabbed a couple of forks. 'At least, enough of it done to be able to get away.'

Oddly, his frown deepened. 'No problems concentrating?'

'I can block everything out when I need to.'

But now she realised she was famished. She reached for the first container instead of him. But he didn't take the fork she'd put on the table for him.

'You're not having any?'

'I already ate.'

She wasn't sorry—all the more for her. 'You chose well.' She licked her lips.

'Uh-huh.' A self-mocking smile curved his lips and then he groaned. 'I should probably—'

'Lie down on the bed,' she said.

His eyes widened.

'I mean, you barely fit in here,' she explained as if it was simple. But she couldn't hold back a playful smile. 'Lying down will probably be the most comfortable place for you in here.'

'Comfortable.' He released a low huff of laughter.

Good. She much preferred it when he smiled.

'I didn't come here for—'

'Yeah, you did,' she said. 'And I'm quite okay with it.'

He toed off his shoes and vaulted up there. She shimmied out of her shorts and tee.

He opened his arms and sighed as she worked her way up his body—loosening his clothes as she went.

'You like appreciation.' She trailed her fingertips across his skin. 'Thanks for dinner,' she breathed.

'You had three bites.'

'I'll have more later. I'm hungry for dessert now.'

Zane had fallen asleep mere moments after she'd ravished him. Stayed asleep for hours. The minx was a fast learner.

He'd wanted to make sure she'd had least had dinner. There was no actual kitchen in her place and he felt hungry at the mere thought of that, and yeah, he knew she ordered in, but he was also sure than sometimes she got too buried in her work to remember. So he'd brought some to her. Turned out *he'd* been the dinner. And he was not complaining.

He *was* surprisingly comfortable in her tiny space, even though, when he stretched right out, his feet hung off the end of her mattress. So he curled up, spooning her. He appreciated the underperforming air-conditioning unit even if it was noisy. It was a calm cocoon in the middle of the sleepless city. He'd been sleepless all week in his quiet, perfectly air-controlled palace.

'Where are you taking me this week?' he asked when she finally stirred as the dawn sun pierced the gap in the curtains. 'You haven't sent an email appointment for my calendar.'

She sighed. 'I don't think I'm going to take you anywhere this week.'

'No?' He shifted and rolled her onto her back so he could see her face. 'You don't want me to meet some logistics operators? Some assistants on the shop floor at the grocery store?'

She shook her head a little glumly. 'I don't think there's much point.'

'You...' He was actually lost for words. She'd given up on trying to convince him to resuscitate Helberg? That meant he'd won. It didn't feel like it. Because he didn't want her to lose her fight.

Her mouth twisted. 'You're going to do whatever you're going to do. What I say isn't going to make a shred of difference.'

That was true, but it wasn't enough. He wanted to prove to her that his plans made good business sense. He wanted her to agree, to admit he was *right*—

His whole body went cold. 'What does this mean for our deal?'

If there was nothing in this for her any more, she might end it early.

She laughed bitterly. 'Nothing matters more than the bet.'

No, that wasn't it. He wanted the time with her. It couldn't be over yet. They had too much fuel still to burn through.

'I should leave you, so you lose the bet,' she said. 'But

it seems I've caught some of your selfishness. My balance is off. You've pointed that out to me.' She looked right into his eyes. 'I still want to further my education with you.'

Immense relief hit. 'That isn't selfish. That's smart.'

Now her lashes lowered. 'I don't think I've been all that smart.'

'What? How so?'

'I've somehow sleepwalked into a life that I didn't plan.' She bowed her head. 'Dad died so unexpectedly.'

Zane swallowed. He didn't much like her father but he got that Skylar had adored him. 'What happened?'

'I was here but I went home most weekends. Worked on the bus both ways so I could hang out with him. I was saving for a new place. I wanted him to have an actual house, you know? His own little bit of land. He wanted that too. Was still working three jobs. And one day, his heart...'

'I'm sorry, Skylar.'

'You know what it's like to lose your dad.'

He shook his head. 'I never had him to begin with.'

The man hadn't wanted to be tied down with the burden of an overactive kid. He'd left when Zane was three. His mother had struggled financially until she could get him into school.

'I think I was lost after he died...he'd been so...'

Authoritarian? Zane bit back his judgment of the man Skylar had loved. And obeyed to the letter.

'I didn't go home again after he'd gone. I couldn't. I buried my grief by being busy at work. I guess I transferred all that loyalty to Helberg...not Reed, the company. I needed to feel indispensable. But I think I also needed the structure it gave me. The familiar discipline and purpose. Rules, you know? Rules to keep you safe. Praise for performing.

Doing an excellent job for everyone but myself.' She bowed her head. 'I'm really tragic.'

Zane didn't know what to say. The old man had been crazy protective and she was sweet and kind and obedient—but spirited beneath. She had a lot of spirit. She'd been stuck up on that balcony like some damned Rapunzel. And Zane hadn't been good enough to be anywhere near her.

Don't you dare...

She was loyal to her father. That was admirable, right?

'You're not tragic.' Zane sighed. 'Maybe he was afraid of losing you. Maybe that's why he held the reins he had on you so tightly. He'd lost his wife and he didn't want to lose you too.'

'He never would have lost me.'

'You'd never have fallen in love? Got married and moved towns?' Zane stilled inside, not wanting to hear her answer. She never would have picked a lover over the wishes of her father.

The past shimmered between them. A moment that should have been nothing. That they should be able to laugh about now. But he couldn't even bring himself to mention it aloud.

'I would have stayed near. I would have done anything...'

Yeah. That old bitterness rippled through him. Even though part of him understood it. Totally. 'You were scared of losing him too. You clung to the things that worked for you both to make you feel secure. He was strict and you were studious. But you don't owe anyone anything now. You've got those savings from your hard work. Your *effort*. But maybe you were so busy putting all your effort into the work you didn't have the energy to explore your own hopes and dreams. Your needs. You do have needs, Skylar.'

Skylar pressed her cheek against her cool pillow. 'You mean I'm a repressed nympho.' She felt hot and prickly inside.

'You should have your own dreams. You should just do what you want, Skylar.'

The trouble was those 'needs' had only turned up the same time as he had. Just as they had when they were teenagers. Before she'd gone back to that boarding school and he'd gone to make it big in the city.

And they were worsening. She needed them to ease off and this conversation really wasn't helping. 'For someone who doesn't like relationships, you're quite the analyst.'

'I'm at a distance and able to observe more dispassionately, I guess.' He cleared his throat.

He was *definitely* at a distance. Deliberately. He kept secrets. Fair enough. She usually did too—by circumstance. There wasn't someone around who she'd talk this personal with. But he was easy to talk to. She'd just told him too much.

That pale blue of his eyes had all but disappeared now and she stared into the depths of his pupils.

'I just want to see you do whatever the hell *you* want,' he said gruffly.

That was how *he* lived. Doing what he wanted. With whomever he wanted.

She'd loved her father but he'd wanted her to be 'good'— by *his* definition. *Don't you dare*...run off and abandon all responsibility. Don't leave him in the lurch. Alone. Like her mother had left them both.

But he'd never encouraged her to be *brave*. He'd never given her alternatives to consider. It had been *his* way... and she'd never had the chance to figure out what she truly wanted to reach for.

She needed to—not just regarding her career, but her personal life as well. Because how she'd been living all these years wasn't enough. She'd lived so long with pressure to succeed, to please her dad, to please her bosses, her colleagues. Working all the hours. But that had been to avoid other parts of life. These last couple of weeks had shown her this, and she was hungry for a lot more. But she had only until Labour Day with Zane. She couldn't think beyond that. So for now, there was the one fantasy she could fulfil. 'I want this weekend away.'

CHAPTER THIRTEEN

JUST AFTER LUNCHTIME on Friday, Skylar passed Bernie on her way down the stairs. He noted her bag and the jacket she'd slung over her shoulder and smiled broadly.

'You're leaving early?' he asked.

For the first time ever. She smiled shyly as she nodded. 'Have a great weekend, Bernie.'

At the airport she drew a breath as Zane introduced her to the liveried crew lined up to greet them in the luxury private lounge. He joked with the pilots, who teased him right back—which made her curious.

'You travel with this crew often?' she asked as they boarded the plush ten-seater cabin, though they were the only passengers on board.

'Whenever I can. They're good. This private charter airline was a spin-off from a large acquisition I made a few years ago.' He took the seat opposite hers. 'They've tripled in size since then. Naturally they love me.'

'So this is your one asset-stripping success story.'

He shot her that smug look. 'One of many, Skylar.'

'You really believe in what you do?'

He cocked his head and a serious gleam entered his expression. 'Yeah, I do. Nothing lasts for ever. Companies come and go—fortune smiles on them one year, then a storm hits. Being able to adapt is a skill not all CEOs have. They don't see the squall coming, they can't course-correct quickly enough.'

'So you lighten their load so they can move faster again?'

'And be agile, yes.'

As much as it galled, she actually believed him. She'd done what he'd told her to the other day. She'd looked at the numbers. Closely. And he was right. She just hadn't wanted to see what it really meant. And even now she still hoped that a massive overhaul wouldn't mean total destruction.

She'd not wanted to think of Zane as a good guy in any way, but that was because of her pride, wasn't it? She'd let their past cloud her judgment of his business practice. She'd disliked his successes—in every arena. Hell, maybe she was jealous. But he was successful for a reason. Some companies actually welcomed his interest—*wanted* him to come in and tell them how to streamline and refocus their businesses.

And if she were honest with herself, it wasn't that galling any more.

She went for an unsubtle subject change. 'How long is the flight?'

He stretched back in his seat and shot her a come-hither look. 'Long enough to give you a very in-depth lesson on the pleasures of the Mile High Club.'

'Does a private jet even count?' she challenged huskily.

'Why, Skylar.' He smirked. 'Do you want the thrill of the crowds on commercial? Are you a closet exhibitionist?'

Apparently she was many things around him. Mostly, she was free—to say what she really thought and do what she really wanted. Because he didn't really care what she thought of him, right? He played up to her little sledges of him but underneath he didn't give a damn. He was purely himself. Although to be fair, she had to admit he was a good listener. She'd talked too much lately but he'd been quietly supportive. And he'd listened to her all those years ago when her mother had left and she'd been sad.

He'd not said anything then either. Just silently offered a few moments of companionship. And a little something sweet as distraction.

He could be kind, in a quiet, understated way. But that silence was also frustrating.

Yet she could ask him for things without worry. He'd tease her about it, but he'd deliver. She knew if she ever asked him to screw her on board a plane alongside hundreds of other passengers, he would. With flair. And yes, that thought had her hot.

There were no 'set lessons' in bed with him. No plan. There was just exploration, discovery, and every experience she had with him was different. And delightful.

On paper, this ought to be the perfect 'benefits' arrangement. She should just keep on enjoying it. Trouble was, it was a little *too* perfect. She was enjoying it all a little *too* much. And he'd made her realise all that she *had* been missing out on. It was a lot—and she wondered what more there was. But in a matter of weeks, this game would be over. Her skin chilled. She gritted her teeth—halting the discomforting direction of her thoughts. She had to forget the future. She had to make the most of it now.

'When does the lesson begin, before or after take-off?' she asked.

'You know it's already started.'

Their plane landed an hour before sundown. A waiting car took them to a stunning villa situated right on a beach. Private and spacious, it showcased stunning views of wide blue skies. Skylar gazed in awe at the powdery pale pink beach and the teal water. It was so transparent that she could see shells and fish and singular grains of that gorgeous sand. The air was balmy and evocative.

'Want to shower and change, then food?' he murmured.

'Yes.'

The bedroom had crisp white linen, an oversize soaking tub and yet more of those stunning views. She stepped into the dress she'd bought specially during the lunch break she'd actually taken two days ago. The floral organza had a deep vee neckline and fitted bodice that then flared into a floor-length skirt, which had a thigh-high split. She didn't bother with shoes. She was relaxed and hedonistic and living in this moment. Only this moment. Because it was the sexiest of summer nights.

She found Zane down by the water's edge, trousers rolled up and paddling in the shallows. He watched as she walked across the powdery sand to meet him and she felt a hot pride when she saw the colour run beneath his skin.

'Nice dress,' he muttered. 'Nice earrings.'

'I made a little effort.' She hitched her skirt and flashed the tiny silk briefs that were the exact shade of the dress.

His eyes actually glazed over. 'And I very much appreciate…'

She paused a couple of feet away, watching him with a coy smile. 'Are you speechless?'

He just lunged for her.

It was another hour before they got to the charcuterie board the discreet staff had left for them. Afterwards, Skylar lay in his arms and listened to the water and let him take her to the stars. Again.

* * *

'Come on, Sleeping Beauty.'

'What?' Skylar rolled onto her side with a moan that deepened into a complete groan when she saw he was fully dressed and standing beside the bed with his hands behind his back. '*Why* are you waking me so early?'

'Because it's Saturday morning, and don't you run three miles every Saturday morning?'

She blinked at him. 'What?'

'There's a group run. Local park. Not far from here.'

Her pulse picked up. 'But I didn't bring my gear.'

He pulled a hand from behind his back and showed her a shoe box. Her brand. Her size.

She gaped at him. 'How did you—'

He whipped out his other hand, dangling a large bag. 'I've got shorts, tee, socks as well.'

'You saw my size at my apartment?'

He shook both box and bag. 'Come on, you don't want to miss it seeing I've gone to all this *effort*.'

He was teasing but this *was* a big effort.

'You have a really big brain, don't you? Big memory.' She took the purchases from him.

'Well, I wasn't sure about underwear.'

'I can make it work.' She chuckled and took the shoes from the box. 'Are you going to run too?'

'Absolutely not.' He turned. 'I'll go find you some electrolytes for after.'

She smiled as she pulled out the shorts and tank he'd got her. He'd even noticed her passion for neon colours.

She hesitated. 'Why did you do this?'

'Because you haven't missed a run in more than two

years and I'm not being the reason for you to break your Saturday-morning streak.'

She stared at him, somewhat taken aback.

'I don't want to stand in the way of things that are important to you. Running is important to you.'

Warmth bloomed in her chest. 'You realise I'm not fast or anything. Like not at all. To be honest I only started running because it was the one way I could get dad to let me out. I took my time—went slow and enjoyed the outdoors.'

His expression turned tender.

'But I'm still slow,' she whispered, a little embarrassed. 'Like, seriously middle to the back of the pack.'

'Thank goodness.' He huffed out an exaggerated sigh of relief. 'It was getting stressful, you being excellent in every bloody thing you do. No way I can compete.'

'Please.' She chuckled at that. '*You* excel at everything.'

He was a natural genius. She'd had to work so hard to get grades half as good as his. But he'd had to work hard too—to overcome his injuries and rebuild his physical strength. So in that they were similar—determined, driven, disciplined.

He winked at her. 'Why, thank you.'

'Ugh.' She gave him a playful shove. 'You were fishing for compliments.'

'And you delivered. Beautifully.' He pressed a quick kiss to her pouting mouth. 'Get ready.'

Zane couldn't wipe the smile from his face as he watched Skylar join the throng of people similarly clad in brightly coloured, dry-wicking tops and shorts. Her smile was infectious, all full-dimpled delight. The couple standing near her smiled back. In seconds she was engaged in conversation, her head cocked as she listened and nodded. She might feel awkward but she was interested in others. She was nice. Curious. Kind.

He'd not considered that watching her run would be arousing. But she was beautiful with her ponytail streaming out behind her, colour in her cheeks and a wide smile on her face as she pushed for a sprint finish alongside some random septuagenarian—totally in her happy place. Zane gripped her water bottle. His chest felt tight, as if he were the one who'd been running—a marathon or more.

She crossed the line smack bang in the middle of the pack—tying with the old guy—just as she'd predicted, but he couldn't help clapping and cheering as if she'd just won Boston. She waved bye to the couple she'd chatted with at the start line, then wove her way through the milling crowd to him. He scooped her into his arms and kissed her.

'I'm all sweaty.' She wriggled in embarrassment but he didn't release her.

'Yeah.' He didn't care. But he stepped back and pulled a couple wrapped pieces of candy from his pocket and offered them to her. 'Raspberry or lemon?'

She looked at the candy in his palm and then up into his eyes. He knew she was remembering that moment in the stairwell so long ago. He was too. And he thought he knew which she'd pick.

'Raspberry.'

Right. The real favourite. Satisfaction and sweet, steamy memory swept over him. 'We'd barely spoken before that afternoon and you just melted in my arms,' he muttered. He'd never forgotten it.

Skylar rocked onto her toes in her new trainers. She'd not expected him to mention that. Certainly not now. But she wanted to hear what he had to say about it.

'You were so beautiful,' he added. 'So hot.'

'So were you.' But then she remembered how badly that moment had ended. She ought to say something now. Apologise for not saying anything then. Her father had been so awful. But before she could say more, he slung his arm around her waist and squeezed.

'Let's go back to the hotel and I'll give you a rub down.'

'Now, there's an offer,' she breathed, both aroused and disappointed.

She wanted to talk about that moment with him. She wanted to work it through. But now he had that charmingly wicked smile on his face and she put that raspberry candy into her mouth. Because *he* didn't open up—that was how he rolled.

'There'll be pancakes, strawberries and cream too,' he drawled. 'And coffee.'

'Stop it.' She pouted at him. 'Or I'll end up falling in like with you.'

He laughed. 'An arrogant prat like me? Impossible.'

But Skylar almost choked on the last of her candy. Because she did like him. She actually, truly did. She wasn't supposed to. The fact that she *didn't* like him was what was meant to have protected her. Because this only about sex. About getting him out of her system for good so she could move forward and be more…normal. Maybe meet another man. But now *that* prospect was horrifying. She didn't *want* anyone else. She never had.

But this was nothing more than a *game* to Zane. He didn't want a relationship. He indulged only in fun *physical* intimacy—he'd been with a heap of women in the past. And she knew it was never emotional. Because he didn't open up. Sure, he'd listened to her prattle on about her past some, offered the smallest of responses. But then he redirected. Hell, he hadn't even mentioned the total bawling out her father had given them both that day just now. Which bothered her so much but she didn't know what to do about it.

Flustered by her inner chaos, she opted for redirection herself. 'What I *really* like is the beach.'

'Then let's go.'

'You want to go on the water?' he called as she walked over the beautiful sand in a scarlet bikini more than an hour later. 'I'll paddle. You'll be tired from your run. You can spot the fish.'

He'd prepped a two-seater ocean kayak with snorkels, masks and flippers on board, plus a stash of water and snacks. As excited as a kid on her first-ever outdoor experience, she scrambled into the front seat and eagerly pointed out all the pretty fish and coral she spotted.

'You didn't do this much even though we grew up near one of the best beaches in the country, did you?' he teased.

'You didn't either,' she pointed out—pausing to see if he'd talk more about back then.

But he just pointed out a turtle she'd missed.

An hour passed as he paddled them along the reef and from cove to cove. Warmed by the sun and tempted by the sea, she precariously clambered upright and dived into the water to cool off. Getting back on board wasn't quite as easy for her to manage. He watched, laughing at her, until in the end he hauled her back with one strong pull. Then he turned the kayak back towards their beach. She saw the sun had passed its zenith. Time was slipping by too quickly. She carried the snorkels and watched him haul the kayak beyond the waterline ahead of her.

'You're bleeding.' She dropped the gear and grabbed his hand.

'It's nothing.' He tried to curl his hand into a fist. 'Just a blister. Go ahead and tease me about having soft hands not used to real hard work.'

But Skylar held his hand in both of hers and forensically inspected it. It wasn't a blister but a deep cut on the inside of his thumb.

'Why didn't you say something?' She fetched a towel and pressed it against the wound. 'You're really hurt.' She lifted the towel but the gash immediately refilled with blood. 'You should have told me. I would have helped.'

'I didn't need your help. Besides, you were enjoying yourself—'

'At your expense—'

'It's not that bad.' He laughed. 'Just a scratch.'

'It's not a scratch, you're *bleeding*.' She applied more pressure on the wound and glared as he winced. 'You know I would have helped if you'd asked. You didn't have to suffer in silence.'

His smile faded. 'Are you seriously mad with me about this?'

'You hold back. *Everything*.'

'What?' His eyebrows shot up. 'You cannot accuse me of holding back in bed.'

'I mean your feelings.'

He stiffened. 'I don't—'

'Have feelings? Right. You're a robot. Who bleeds. You could talk to me, you know. About anything. I wouldn't mind. But you won't. You can't even express a little literal pain to me, let alone anything actually—' She broke off as she registered his shuttered expression.

She'd gone off. And now she was mortified. She stalked up the beach to the villa, fossicked for a sticking plaster in the small first-aid kit she always had in her pack, then turned back to find him right behind her. She handed the plaster to him.

'I won't offer to put it on for you,' she said. 'Heaven forbid you let someone tend to your wounds.'

He took the plaster meekly. 'Thank you.'

She watched him ruin one plaster. Handed him another. Watched him ruin that one too. Which gave her time to think. To realise her mistake. He didn't talk to her about anything deeply private because he didn't *want* to. Because, as she well knew, this wasn't a relationship. It was an arrangement. And while she might've spoken to him about stuff, that didn't mean he then had to do the same. Talking had been her choice. *Not* talking was his. She had to respect that.

'You do it,' he said gruffly when she tried to hand him a fourth plaster. 'It's too awkward a position for me to manage.'

He sat on the edge of the bed and she knelt to wrap the plaster around his thumb with quick, matter-of-fact ease.

He cleared his throat. 'You think I'm…'

'I think you're okay,' she said softly. Biggest understatement ever. 'I think you're kind. And I think…' She trailed off and shook her head. 'It doesn't really matter what I think.'

Zane gazed down at her. Speechless. Because what she thought did matter to him. And that realisation made him motionless as well as speechless. It shouldn't matter. Until this second, he would've argued it didn't…but it really did. This wasn't like their flirt-tipped verbal swordplay. Or a caustic analysis of their differing views on Helberg. This challenge went deeper.

She was bothered by his silence. And that bothered him.

That first night in his orchard, he hadn't much cared at all—he'd thought it had been his chance to assuage their out-of-control chemistry. And that chance had been extended. He still didn't really *care* though, right? But he was *concerned*.

Surely not saying anything about a stupid small cut that he'd barely noticed was a problem? He'd wanted her to have a good time out there on the reef. Hell, he'd been having a good time. Even with that little bit of pain—it was a little price to pay for the pleasure of seeing her entranced by the sea life.

But now that nothing of a wound throbbed like his thumb had been sliced off completely. Worse, an ache pressed inside him and he couldn't pinpoint the source. He'd put up with physical pain in his leg for years but this was different. He needed to soothe it. Soothe them both. *Silence* them both.

Because talking was pointless. It was action that mattered. Always.

He cupped her face and held her so she couldn't slip away from him and kissed her gently. Then a little less gently, and he leaned back so he could watch that smoky surrender enter her eyes. Then he kissed her everywhere.

And said nothing.

CHAPTER FOURTEEN

SKYLAR STRETCHED OUT her warm, achy muscles. It had been another magical night of tease and sensuality... She blinked drowsily and realised the morning was only *almost* perfect. Zane wasn't lying beside her. She sat up. He was probably taking an early-morning swim. Which was fine. A little space was probably good.

Relax and enjoy it.

But her nerves were brittle and she suddenly felt a wave of warning. She tried to push the panic away—not ruin this moment by panicking about everything ending. Labour Day was a while away and she was here *now*, she could settle for this. It was already more than she'd ever had.

She got out of bed and shrugged on a silk robe. Glancing out the window, she saw he wasn't in the pool. She wandered from the bedroom into the lounge to check the beach view. That's when she registered the softly playing music. She followed the sound—upstairs. Once she hit the second floor she stopped at the open door, unable to believe her eyes. There were tall windows with even more expansive views over that amazing teal water, but Skylar's attention was completely absorbed by Zane. Wearing only boxers, he was seated at a sleek piano. She watched the muscles rippling across his back as he played. Still and silent, she listened until the last note had faded. And when it had? That's when she lost it.

'Are you *kidding* me?' She stalked towards him. 'Of all the—'

'What?' Startled, he spun and lifted his hands like she was pointing a gun at him. 'Did I wake you? I was playing softly. I didn't think you'd be able to hear from the bed.'

She walked towards him. 'I can't believe *you* were really playing that.'

'Who else would it have been?' He grinned.

'A paid professional?' she muttered. 'Like you're not already...'

'Already what?'

'Attractive enough. Gorgeous face. Fit body. Successful.'

His eyes widened. But he joked, 'Don't forget outrageously wealthy.'

'Right, should have put that first. Let's not forget wickedly amusing...a foil to mask the moodiness of a lost soul.'

'Just irresistible, right?'

'Right. And now you're a ridiculously talented musician as well.' She shook her head. 'I think I hate you.'

'You think? You're not sure? You were definite before. So that's definitely progress.'

She shook her head. 'You don't want me to like you.'

'Touché.' He smiled, almost contrite. 'Didn't you notice the music room in my penthouse?'

'I don't think we've made it into your music room.'

'Right.' He chuckled again. 'Another lesson.'

'Seriously.' She was so grumpy with him. 'Is there *nothing* you can't do?'

He pulled a wry face. 'Express my feelings, apparently.'

She sighed and walked towards him. 'I shouldn't have said all that yesterday. I was just tired. You don't have to share anything if you don't want to. Not to me. Or anyone. Or anything.'

'We're spending a lot of time together,' he said slowly. 'I guess it's inevitable we'd be curious about more than...'

'What turns each other on,' she said.

She followed his gaze down to his hands. The plaster on his thumb was still in place. Obviously no hindrance to his performance.

'I've been playing since I was a kid,' he said.

She shook her head. 'I call BS. We lived in the same apartment building for years. Was there even room for a piano in your place? *Surely* I would've heard you practice.'

'Not when I had an old second-hand electronic keyboard and tinny headphones. No one else heard anything.'

Her heart twisted. If she didn't know this, then she didn't really know him at all. 'But when did you have *time*? You were so busy getting strong again. Then doing all your on-line trading things all while acing your studies... How is it possible that you got so good at this?'

He half swivelled back to the piano and played an arpeggio with one hand. 'When my leg ached I'd go through my scales.'

'Distraction?' She perched on the piano stool next to him, unable to resist the need to be nearer to him. To touch.

'Discipline. It kept me focused. My leg hurt all the time. I had several operations through my teens. Eventually it became like a meditation. A place to go to when I needed respite from everything else that was going on.'

She paused, processing all that. It was about the most he'd ever told her about his life. But one thing leapt out at her. 'So you need respite now?'

He hesitated. 'I guess.' He pressed down the keys. 'I couldn't sleep.'

Skylar made herself stay silent. If he wanted her to know *why* he'd been unable to rest, he would tell her. She wasn't going to ask. But it killed her not to.

He nudged her shoulder with his. 'I can see you holding back your questions.'

She smiled and opted for an easy one. 'Please don't tell me you composed that piece.'

He laughed. 'No, that was Debussy.' He glanced at her. 'French composer.'

'I know who Debussy was.'

'Yeah. Of course you do. Brains as well as beauty.'

Not *so* clever. Stupid actually. Stupidly falling for the man she'd once thought she hated. The crush who'd crushed her. The one she couldn't physically resist. And when his stupid bet was over, he would destroy the one constant she had left in her life. Her job. The one she wasn't sure she even wanted any more. He would walk out of her life. And she wouldn't know what to do with herself. She didn't know what to do with herself right now. But she knew for sure he had a soul. No one who could play like that didn't.

'You worked so hard. It really matters to you, doesn't it?' he said quietly.

'Helberg changed my life.' And she wasn't sure it had been for the better any more. But she'd never dreamed a different route. She'd promised her father she'd follow the path he'd outlined—to a better life, right? And if she didn't, she'd end up alone. Only that's where she was anyway, for all her loyalty and duty.

'Yeah,' he muttered. 'He changed mine too.'

Glancing up, she saw bleakness in his eyes. 'Zane—'

'I want you to understand,' he interrupted her before she told him he didn't have to tell her anything. He knew he didn't have to tell her but right now it mattered that she not think him completely shallow and pettily vindictive. He needed her to know. He couldn't hold it down any more.

'You know I went for one of his scholarships. I imagine the process didn't change over the years—you would have had an interview with the great man himself too, right?'

She nodded. 'I was so nervous.'

'Because you'd been told it was such a life-changing opportunity.'

'Yes.' She stared at him.

'I was too young to really appreciate that. Too self-involved. I just wanted to read the things that interested me. I didn't have anything to say to that blustery man and I didn't care. So I came across as a sullen smart-ass.'

'Surely he would have seen through that—'

'Perhaps. But he wanted performers. Articulate and polite and full of adulation. *Don't you know how to smile, boy?* He just wanted someone who'd smile when he was told to, who'd make Reed Helberg look good.'

'How old were you?'

'Eleven.'

Her eyes widened. 'That's so much younger than—' She took a breath. 'I was fifteen when I got a scholarship to that boarding school.'

'They took you on a tour to get your hopes up, right?'

'Yeah. It was huge. All those playing fields and...' Something dawned in her eyes. 'You didn't want to go,' she guessed softly. 'You didn't *want* to win it.'

Yeah, he'd always known she was smart.

'Leave the beach? Home?' He shook his head. 'And I saw those other boys there. I think you'd call them arrogant prats. Entitled and lacking in empathy.'

'Not all of them were like that. At least not all the time.'

'Right. Because you made so many friends there?'

She stared at him. 'Okay, I'll admit Danielle's about the only one.'

'Yeah.' He played another chord. 'Reed's rejection was instant and brutal, and on the long drive home my mother grew increasingly upset.'

'She must've been disappointed for you.'

Zane stopped playing for a moment while he pushed back the pain he'd long tried to hold down. He didn't want to tell her this, but nor did he want her thinking it was only out of shallow spitefulness that he wanted Helberg. It cut so much deeper than money.

'I didn't understand how much she wanted me to go away to that school.' He cleared his throat. 'I was too much, I guess. A scamp of a small boy. In trouble when I was bored—which was all the time in school. The teachers accelerated me but I was still a problem. She didn't have the energy to cope with me.'

He'd been too young to understand just how hard she worked. How tired she must have been dealing with him. Because he hadn't been easy. 'She was in tears. And she lost it. She shouted at me for...' *Everything.* He swallowed. 'She missed the traffic light.'

'That was when you had the accident? On your way back?'

He'd taken the brunt—pinned in the car while his mother had been able walk free. And then everything was worse. So much worse. 'I became even more of a burden.'

Medical bills. Constant hospital appointments. And no fancy boarding school to give her any respite from him.

'Zane—'

'I'd failed.' So he'd never failed again. He didn't lose. Ever. He worked and worked and worked until he won. Once he'd decided on a target, that was it. 'She was upset because of me. Distracted because of me. If I hadn't failed that interview, it wouldn't have happened. The accident was—'

'An *accident*,' Skylar said firmly. 'If anything, your mother could have taken a moment to calm down before driving.'

'We had to get home quickly because she had to get to work. It wasn't her fault.'

'Okay,' Skylar said. 'But it certainly wasn't yours either.'

He shook his head. He'd never forgotten his mother's distress. He'd never wanted to make her—or anyone—that upset again. Not with his failings. Or his demands.

'My grandfather came and stayed briefly. He told me I needed to keep it together. Not bother her. She already had to work hard enough and now there were my medical bills on top of everything. I had to be strong.'

'What about your father? Did he ever help?'

Zane looked at her. 'My mere existence was too much for him. He cleared off when I was three.'

He'd worked hard. He'd absorbed the pain. Learned to be quiet about it. Then worked to get stronger. He'd suppressed everything—including his own emotion—to protect his mother because he knew he'd let her down. He'd cost her the freedom that scholarship would have given her. And he'd learned to damn well smile and mask it all. *Without* Helberg.

'I smiled and acted like nothing ever touched me. Nothing ever bothered me. Nothing ever *hurt*. I can hide hurt, Skylar.' It had become habit.

'Yes.' She looked troubled. Almost guilty.

That moment in the stairwell just after her father had found them flashed before him. When she'd stood silently, letting him take the blame. Letting him be verbally abused. Not speaking up.

He'd hidden his hurt then too. Because he *had* been hurt. The best moment of his life till then had turned atrocious in seconds. He pushed it away and pivoted to what should have been his main point all along.

'I never forgot, never *forgave* Reed Helberg. He made a snap judgment and didn't change his mind about me no matter what I did from then on. I know his opinion shouldn't matter yet it always did.' Zane had channelled his anger towards Helberg. It had been easiest to. 'No one person should have that much power over some kid's life. Why choose just *one* lucky recipient? Why change only one student's life?' The man had been so damned wealthy—until he'd begun to run his company into the ground with a series of bad choices. 'What about all the others? Why not lift the performance of the whole damn school instead of scooping out that one stellar student and sending them somewhere supposedly better.'

Skylar stared at his hands. 'You're the anonymous donor behind the new gym at our old school.'

He shot her surprised look. 'You know there's a new gym?'

'I'm still on the email list for the newsletter.'

'Of course you are.' He blinked.

'What about the new science lab?'

'That too,' he mumbled. 'And the music room.'

'Anything else? A library?'

'A physical rehab centre at the health clinic in town,' he muttered. 'For kids and people who need to rebuild strength after accidents like mine.'

'And that's anonymous too?'

He had to drop his gaze from hers. 'I call in there sometimes. But I don't want my name over anything. It's not about me.'

'So you make out like everything's a bit of a joke. That you don't care. But you donate to all those charity things. Just not publicly.'

'I don't want people to come to me so desperate for my support that they'll do almost anything I want.' A ripple of guilt went down his spine.

'You don't let anyone get that close,' she said softly. 'You've never trusted anyone with the truth of how you actually feel. You didn't take comfort from your family.'

'I didn't need comfort,' he said. 'I could take care of myself.'

'*Everyone* needs comfort.'

'No, they don't.'

'Right, that's why you support a rehab clinic for kids. Why you go visit them and encourage them. Because they don't need comfort.'

'That's different.'

'Why? Because they're not as tough as you? Not as capable?'

'They're far braver than I ever was.'

'Yet you say you didn't need comfort.'

He rolled his shoulders. 'Don't, Skylar.'

'I'm not judging you, Zane.'

'No?'

'No.' She sighed. 'We all do our best, but we all screw up sometimes. And most of us admit we need help sometimes. But not you. You won't ever stop or ask for help. Or take a step back and say, *I'm tired.*'

'I'm tired.' He paused. 'Of this conversation.'

He didn't know why he'd thought it would be a good idea to start this. Why it would help in any way at all. Because now she was looking at him with soft sadness in her eyes and he did not want her pity. He didn't want her feeling *that* for him.

'Where's your mother now?' she asked.

'Florida. Fiercely independent. Won't retire even though I bought her a condo and made arrangements. She cancelled them. She doesn't touch the account I opened for her.'

He wanted to take care of her and she wouldn't let him and it rubbed everything that was raw inside and now he *really* regretted saying everything he had in the last half hour.

'Maybe she feels like she doesn't deserve your help because of what happened.'

'*I* caused that crash.'

'It was an *accident.*'

'*Stop.*'

'You're invoking your safe word when we're just talking?'

Yeah. Because he didn't talk. He shouldn't have said any of this to her.

'So you do everything good quietly. And everything wicked with a smile.'

'I make the tiniest of differences,' he growled. 'And I'm no saint. I bought the house of my dreams on the beach that I love and I have my Manhattan penthouse with a spectacular view. And you know I like my personal pleasures too.' He drew in a sharp breath. 'Money and power corrupts. Who's to say it hasn't corrupted me?'

'Because you know what it is to be desperate and you wouldn't take advantage of anyone in that state.

'No?' He looked at her bitterly. 'Wouldn't I take advantage of someone desperately wanting to convince me to do something about something they cared about?'

'You haven't taken advantage of *me*.' She looked put out.

'I'm not so sure about that.'

He'd been pleased to find her literally caught in his orchard and needing his help. He'd been pleased that she couldn't get away. For a moment there, he'd even toyed with the fanciful idea of not helping her, so she'd be trapped in his garden for always. Because that old chemistry had flared. And then he'd used that stupid bet—all but engineered her loyalty to the company to spend more time with him. Because she'd always been in the back of his mind. The one he couldn't have. The one he wanted more than any other. And he didn't know what he felt worse about— engineering their fling, or the fact that he *still* wanted her so badly.

'*I'm* the one who pushed for us to sleep together again,' she said. 'I asked. I took. Don't act as if it were all your idea.'

Yeah, but she just wanted some 'experience.' He'd not been good enough for her back then. He'd been a *distraction*. Maybe that's all he was now too. Because even more important to her was her desire to save Helberg. Once this bet was done, she'd continue with her workaholic ways without him. The thought of all that reality bit hard. *Unsatisfied.* He was still *so* unsatisfied.

'Kiss me then,' he muttered gruffly. 'If that's what you want.'

She lifted his hand from the keys and pressed her lips to that raw spot on the inside of his thumb. The small thing that still hurt.

Her touch was too gentle and it wasn't enough. He was still greedy. He slipped his hands around her and drew her onto his lap. He would take this now. Only now.

And then they would be done.

CHAPTER FIFTEEN

ZANE'S MOOD DROPPED like a stone when he realised it was early and he was alone. They were flying back to Manhattan tonight and he really didn't want to have woken alone at this hour. They'd spent most of yesterday in bed after that time at the piano. It still hadn't been enough. And now she was gone. He went hunting for her. Found her in the lounge. She'd positioned a wide armchair to catch the first rays of the sun.

'You're working?' He checked his stride when he saw her laptop. 'I thought you'd got everything done before we left.'

He hadn't realised she'd brought her computer. Admittedly he'd brought his but he hadn't opened it. Hell, he hadn't *remembered* he had it till now. But here she was, up at stupid o'clock working—mentally back in Manhattan already, and was he actually feeling jealous that her attention was elsewhere?

He gritted his teeth at the bitter irony. Usually he was the one too busy to be sociable over breakfast—the one avoiding extended intimacy with a conveniently timed meeting. But not now. Now he wanted her back in his bed. Warm and willing and fully focused on him.

'I'm just doing a favour for Avery,' she muttered. Her gaze remained trained on the screen in front of her.

Zane was the one who didn't get distracted—he didn't prioritise a lover over work, but today *Skylar* wasn't. Because work was totally her priority. As it should be his.

They clearly felt differently. Hell, he actually *felt*—and not good. The realisation that she wasn't as into this thing between them as he was, was sharply—what? Painful? Suddenly he was pissed on several levels.

'She's in logistics,' Skylar added, oblivious to the tornado brewing inside him. 'Such a sweetheart. One of her kids is really into distance running. Way faster than me.'

His overly possessive outrage worsened. Of course she knew all this about the woman and her family—she was gently curious and she remembered everything. That one-to-one kindness of hers was genuine. But it was also universal. Belatedly he bitterly realised that her listening to him yesterday morning hadn't been anything special to *her*—she did that for *all* of her work associates. But for him it had been decidedly unique.

He felt exposed. And even though he'd told her all he had about Helberg, she still wanted that damned company to be rescued. She was doing work for the bloody thing right now and he knew it was irrational of him to be angry about that, but he was. And dealing with it, he *wasn't*.

His old pain hadn't affected her view of the company at all. Because she still cared about all the people she worked with. *They* mattered to her more than anything *he'd* shared with her. And that was fair enough. He was nothing more than a deal to her.

Except he was bothered. Badly.

And nothing soothed it this time. Not the swim he had with her when she'd finally finished. Not the leisurely lunch they shared. Not the last few hours they'd spent in that magnificent bed—he'd carried her there, determined to have her attention solely on him. And he'd succeeded.

Only then he realised the extent of his mistake.

He didn't do this. He didn't spend night after night with one woman and certainly didn't go on holiday with her. He didn't laze about, talking of too much that was too private. He'd never let anyone get to him like this—God, didn't it serve him right to be finally interested in a woman only to find she wasn't really interested in him.

But she was beneath his skin—and there was part of him wanting her to *stay*. His heart pounded. He couldn't let her get any deeper.

The fact was they were *never* going to agree on what ought to be done with Helberg. Nothing had changed there. Nor would it. So this whole game they had going—and it *was*, he reminded himself, a game—was pointless. No point in continuing the arrangement. Because he was angry. And uncomfortable—he'd told her too much.

The demise of Helberg would devastate her. There was no disentangling how this whole mess had begun. He'd wanted her—now he'd had her he wanted more. But she just wanted to protect Helberg, and getting some sexual experience had merely been a bonus on the side.

So this whole situation was only going to worsen in every way.

There was only one option left to him. And he couldn't get back to Manhattan quickly enough.

Bitterly—weakly—he stalled until the last few minutes when his driver was en route to her tiny apartment.

'You're free of any obligation to me, the deal's off,' he said quietly.

She twisted in her seat. Her expression confused. 'What does that mean?'

'You don't need to be my date any more. It's not necessary.'

Her eyes widened. 'Has something happened with Helberg? Someone else made an offer?'

Right. Of course her first thought was about the company. Not him.

He shook his head. 'I've reconsidered my position,' he said coolly. 'I can just stop dating for the rest of the time and still win Helberg. As long as I'm not seen with another date then I'm still in it.'

He didn't know what he was going to do about the stupid bet. Right now he just needed space from her.

'You don't want to go on any more dates with me?'

Bingo. 'It's not fair of me to hold you to the bargain when you've already conceded.'

Skylar could hardly hear over the thundering of her pulse in her ears but it sounded a lot like he was ending their deal early. Way too early. She needlessly fiddled with her bag, needing a reason not to look into his eyes. 'How noble of you to want to play fair.'

She'd known it would end but she'd thought she had a few more weeks. Labour Day, right?

'I don't want to hurt—'

'You haven't,' she interrupted him quickly. 'This was always a temporary thing.'

'I know,' he clipped. 'I meant about dismantling Helberg. I can't change my view on what needs to be done there.'

'Right. Of course.' She released a tight breath. 'To be honest, I knew that.'

He hadn't changed. But to her horror, she realised *she* had. Not in regard to Helberg—in regard to *him*. She didn't want this fling to end early. Because spending all this time with him—getting to know him properly, beyond the chemistry that had blinded her for so long—had changed her.

She hadn't known that terrible accident had occurred right after his awful scholarship interview. That he'd been so young, a wary, too-intelligent boy who hadn't wanted to leave his home. A boy who'd already been rejected by his own father and who then realised that his mother too didn't seem to want him around. Skylar knew how deep, how irrevocable that kind of hurt was. To have a parent who wasn't interested. Who left.

No wonder he'd blamed Reed Helberg—because it was far easier to hate him for it all than to put it on his parents, who she knew he still loved.

She totally understood that feeling. Unlike him, she'd wanted to escape—only she hadn't. Not even now. She still worked for that complete pressure.

Her father had humiliated Zanc that crazy afternoon when they'd kissed so passionately in the stairwell. But she'd said nothing—she'd just stood there and let Zane take all the blame. It might've stung at thc time but it wouldn't have bothered Zane the same as the others. He probably laughed about it—if he ever thought of it at all. And he had what he wanted now—his success and that beautiful home on the beach. But he was very, very alone. That was how he wanted it—or so he proclaimed. But now she knew the scars on his thigh weren't anywhere as deep as the ones inside.

'Why was it okay for us to be together this weekend but not for longer?' she couldn't stop herself from asking. 'What's changed?'

He shook his head. 'Nothing's changed. That's the point.'

But he should have people in his life—for longer than the few nights he allowed.

'You might have a lonely few weeks,' she muttered. 'Not dating anyone.'

'I think I can handle it,' he muttered dismissively.

But he didn't *have* to. Her heart pounded harder. 'You don't want company?' She tried to keep it light. But she was angry with him for waiting until the last possible moment to tell her. To give her no time to process or to argue. But it slipped out anyway. 'You don't think we could just keep on seeing each other like this?' She could handle a bit longer. It was only sex after all. An affair that she didn't want to be over yet.

'No.' He stared just beyond her, slightly pale given the last few days in the sun.

No. Instant, flat rejection.

'I don't want to,' he added.

As if she hadn't got the memo already.

It hurt so much more than it should. *Stupid, Skylar.* This was only a game and apparently for him it was no longer fun. Was he *bored*? After all, they'd had a few more dates than one.

She shouldn't have asked. She'd sounded pathetic and needy. She forced a smile to cover up and was so, so glad the chauffeur had pulled up outside of her apartment. 'Sure. Of course.' She opened the door and as she scrambled to get out of the car, she muttered, 'I guess you're going to be busy.'

CHAPTER SIXTEEN

ZANE STOOD ALONGSIDE GRACE, unable to sling his arm around her shoulder like they'd agreed. He'd managed to stand with his hand hovering at her back on their way into the restaurant and he knew the photos had been uploaded directly to socials. Even so, he'd endured dinner with her at the restaurant just below the rooftop bar they were now heading to for the final part of the evening. He'd hated every second but he was determined to see it through. There would be more photos taken at the bar, which would ensure there would be no doubt—Zane deMarco was back to his one-date wonder ways.

'At least *try* to smile,' Grace murmured as they moved past the next photographer.

Tonight's event was a frivolous summer celebration. No worthy high society charity do, this was a vibrant night offering excess and excitement and some new EP from some famous music producer. One that high-profile influencers posted live on their social media accounts. All pumping music, vibrant lights, short dresses, tight shirts, sparkles and skin…pure festival vibe. The rooftop club and bar was packed while the famous DJ dropped his best beats.

Zane shot his senior analyst a rueful look. 'Thanks for this. I'm going to push off shortly.'

Grace didn't even try to convince him to change his mind. 'Thanks for getting me in here. I've always wanted to see this bar.'

'Enjoy.' He knew she'd be fine—she was on track for a fantastic night. Whereas he was officially over people and parties. He wanted nothing more than to be alone. He'd pay his driver triple time and go back to the beach tonight. He might have to take a bottle of whisky with him.

But he couldn't resist a moment to check the stunning view of the Hudson River and the city lights, but three steps along he came face-to-face with Cade Landry.

'Hey.' Zane braced.

'Who's that?' Cade jerked his head towards Grace, currently stalking her way through to the dance floor. 'I thought you were seeing some petite brunette who works at Helberg.' Cade's eyes narrowed. 'Which is pretty interesting, given everything.'

'Didn't work out,' Zane said shortly.

'No?' Cade lifted his glass with a smirk. 'That isn't her heading towards us right now?'

Zane whirled and scanned the balcony, instantly spotting her petite frame amongst the revellers.

He'd died and gone to hell.

The scarlet minidress stopped his heart. The look in her eyes ripped it from his chest. Five days since he'd seen her. Five interminable days and endlessly restless nights.

She'd not been in touch and he'd been doing everything to keep himself distracted and not succumb to the temptation of calling her. He'd left the city for a couple of nights just to stop himself. It was while he was away then that he'd made this plan. Because he needed to be clear of *everything* she was associated with.

Quickly he turned back to Cade. 'I'm out of the bet. I don't want Helberg. You and Adam carry on without me.'

Cade's jaw dropped. 'You're—'

'Done. I've dated two women since the bet started. There'll be more in the next few days. I'm out. Completely.'

He didn't explain further. He just had to get away. From Skylar. From trying to explain it to *her* without…he didn't know what.

He pushed through the crowds and got to the elevator, hitting the buttons to get him down. Out. Away. The lift didn't come and the tightness in his chest worsened. He'd take the stairs. He weaved through the crowds again, no relief from that image of her in his mind, and as he turned the corner she was there. Right in his path, as if she'd just been waiting for him all along.

'Why are you running away so early?' she said.

Because he couldn't stand seeing her. Especially not in that scarlet minidress. The long sleeves and high neck were made of something see-through while a silk slip the same colour covered her best bits beneath—but only just. It was playful and provocative as hell. Her hair was in that high ponytail and his ruby earrings sparkled in the light. But it was her eyes he really couldn't handle seeing. Not the gleaming anger in them.

Why was *she* angry? *He* was the angry one.

'What about your date?' she asked over the top of the thudding music. 'Are you just going to leave her alone here?'

His chest tightened even more. She was concerned for his *date*? She wasn't jealous at all—not even the *slightest*?

'She's fine,' he said tightly. Grace wouldn't be at all bothered that he'd vanished. He desperately needed to get to the beach and down that bottle of whisky. Maybe two.

'Are you deliberately throwing the bet with a fake date?' Skylar stood right in front of him and she was taller because she was wearing high heels the colour of her dress.

He gritted his teeth. He did not want to answer that question.

'Don't you want Helberg any more?' She followed up.

Of course she'd ask about Helberg. It really was her priority. And of course that was exactly why he'd decided to step back from it completely. And of course tonight's bloody date was fake. 'Right.'

Her eyes widened. 'Why not?' She drew a sharp breath. 'What's changed?'

'The price,' he muttered harshly. 'Pushing up. It's one I can no longer pay.'

'You've decided it's going to cost you too much?'

'Something like that.' He didn't want to talk about this. He didn't want her to know the truth. So he fudged. 'There are safer investment options.'

'Safer,' she echoed.

Why had he ever wanted the stupid company—why had it mattered so much that he be that one to break it apart? He couldn't remember why he'd felt that so intensely any more. Everything had been superseded by something else. Some*one*. And she was just staring at him now, her brown eyes deep and doubtful and angry.

'I don't care about what happened with Helberg any more,' he growled. 'That's so long ago now. Maybe I can even thank him for motivating me to succeed. I probably wouldn't have had that fire without his...damned judgment.'

She was still for a second and he tensed up even more.

'So you've made peace with it?' She blinked slowly. 'Good for you.'

It wasn't 'good.' He simply had no choice. Even though he knew she was only interested in him physically, he couldn't be the one to break Helberg up. It would still happen, but at least it wouldn't be him. It wasn't that he cared about the stupid company—he cared too much for her. And while she'd finally acknowledged the problems with the company, she still didn't want it to happen. And he didn't want to be the one to cause her that hurt.

Irritated with his weakness for her, his control slipped. 'Why are you here tonight? This isn't your scene.' He cleared his throat as a fierce glint flashed in her eyes. 'How did you even get in?'

She didn't move. For a moment he didn't think she'd heard him.

'You should leave.' He wanted to leave. 'It's over between us, Skylar.' He had to remind himself. 'I've moved on.'

Her lips slowly curved. 'You think I came here tonight to see you?'

Hadn't she? 'You're wearing the earrings I gave you.' His voice rose as his rage rose, because she looked stunning—make-up, jewellery, the things she'd never bothered with before. Was she here to meet other *men*? 'You've made an *effort*—'

'Yeah, I did,' she snapped. 'I made an effort. For *me*.'

The music was beating so loudly Skylar couldn't be sure he'd even heard her, but it didn't matter. She turned and took her shredded heart and turned on her heel while she could remain upright. She needed to breathe. Just breathe. Just for a moment. Because in this instant she couldn't keep it together, not for a second longer. And she needed to.

He'd *crushed* her. Blindly she walked—missing the exit, just heading to another part of the balcony bar. She'd seen his arrival at that restaurant with the tall blonde on her social media. It had popped up practically in real time. The strangest ice-cold rage had overcome her. She'd dressed, jumped in a cab and stalked with fierce confidence straight past the security guys at the door, who'd just waived her through. She'd had to see for herself if he was throwing the bet or if that date was *real*. Yet finding out it was fake hadn't given her any relief, because seeing him again had ripped the barely formed scab from a wound she'd not acknowledged was so damned *deep*. She missed him. She wanted him. So very much.

She made it ten paces before stopping. It didn't make sense. *None* of it made sense to her. What *was* he doing? Why? Was he really over a lifetime of anger? She needed to understand properly. Turning, she retraced her steps.

He was standing where she'd left him. His head was bowed as he leaned against the pillar and his expression almost yanked her already battered heart out of her chest.

'Zane...' she whispered.

He jerked his head up, somehow hearing her, and that haunted expression was instantly wiped. 'What are you doing?' he said harshly.

'What are *you* doing?' She glared at him. 'You're at a fabulous club with a stunning, beautiful woman and you look freaking miserable. Answer me honestly—are you okay?'

He stared at her. Stunned. And said nothing.

'No?' She stepped up close to him. 'You know what I think? I think you've spent your life suppressing your own needs and protecting people from your true feelings.'

Exactly the same as she had. She'd been so good for so long. She'd done everything expected of her—and more—

for her whole damned life. Even when she no longer actually had to. And it was enough already.

'You think I suppressed my needs around *you*?' he mocked harshly.

'I'm not talking about sex.' She breathed hard. 'At least, not *only* sex.'

He stared at her.

'You ended this with me before you needed to because what, you actually opened up for five minutes? You got uncomfortable with that?' She shook her head. 'The thing is, you've got more to offer a woman than you think.'

'Skylar—'

'I get that you don't want *me*. I get that.' She stretched up as tall as she could and spoke furiously, right in his ear. 'I thought you were totally cold beneath that playboy exterior. That superficial charm masked an empty shell. That you took things apart because you're not whole and you can't stand to see other things complete.'

His nostrils flared.

'But you're not,' she said huskily. 'You brought me my favourite food, remembered the things I like to do. You supported me in my one hobby…that wasn't all part of the game. That was *you*. You're a caring, kind guy. You have more than great sex to offer someone, you know? You should have a person in your life.'

She really wanted to be that person, and while she could accept his decision that she wasn't, she desperately hoped he might change his mind. That he might be hiding so much more—same as she.

But he just stared down at her. 'I thought you said I was an arrogant prat,' he said roughly.

She rocked back onto her heels. 'The fact is you know me better than anyone else, but I know *you* too. I know how you can hide hurt, Zane. You even *told* me how good you are at it. I think you're afraid, and I don't blame you because you took some rough blows when we were young. But you can't hide it for ever. It'll rise,' she said, her voice catching. 'Eventually it'll become impossible to ignore. And all the partying in the world, all the money you can make, won't be distraction enough. And when you finally realise that maybe you *do* have the courage to face it, and let someone in, it might just be too late.'

He still didn't move. The man was ice. He wanted to stay that way. And it was too late for *her* already. Her shredded heart broke right in two. She blinked, furious with her loss of emotional control in the face of his rigidity. But that's where they were different now, right? She *let* herself feel. He still didn't.

'You should go home,' he said gruffly.

'Screw that.' She lifted her chin with a defiant sniff, determined to mask up again. 'I'm going dancing.'

CHAPTER SEVENTEEN

JEALOUSY STORMED THROUGH Zane at the thought of her on a dance floor with someone else. He made himself walk. Away. Not go caveman and scoop her up and storm out of there with her hanging upside down and screaming over his shoulder. Much as he wanted to.

This possessiveness was intolerable. He instructed his driver to floor it and keep driving. He didn't want to go back to his penthouse. It was tainted with memories of her. As was the beach house. But he needed to go somewhere. A momentary stop at a liquor store helped...eventually. Hours later, he was where he needed to be. Alone and by the ocean and more than halfway through a bottle of whisky.

Not that he felt any better for it.

He tossed the bottle off the balcony, irritated. He didn't do this. He never drank alone. Never tried to numb pain with substance abuse. He endured—and he could handle this too, right? This was nothing.

But it wasn't nothing. It was agony. And it was awful.

This was the thing he couldn't do. *Relationships*. Fun, yes. For sure. But that had become a hollow satisfaction, whereas his satisfaction with Skylar was anything but hollow. It was everything.

But she didn't want a relationship either. She didn't want

to make that *effort*. Sex was 'easy' with him and all she'd wanted was the experience he could offer. The 'learning' she'd not had for years for whatever unfathomable reason. And he was a safe choice because he didn't want relationships either—he was a one-date wonder after all...

Except maybe now he wasn't.

And the bitter irony was he meant little more than nothing to her. It was only Helberg she held in her heart. For her father. That was why she'd come looking for him. And he'd used it, hadn't he, to manipulate her into his little game. Because having sex with her the once hadn't been enough.

Heaven knew he would never have enough.

Groaning, he stumbled downstairs to the cabinet and abandoned his noble attempts to endure pain. He couldn't do it any more. He needed an anaesthetic and whisky was the only available option.

Hours later, his head was absolutely killing him. So was his heart. Every damn beat reverberated the pain around his body. It *sucked*.

He stood beneath the shower and flicked it to cold. He leaned against the wall and closed his eyes and endured the freezing temperatures. Regretting everything.

Pure self-inflicted punishment. His relentless thoughts of Skylar only made it worse. They'd tumbled into lust the second they'd had the chance. Both back when they were both teens and again when he'd found her in his garden. Both times they'd barely spoken before the chemistry between them had instantly exploded—out of control and unstoppable.

Her father had broken them apart and torn strips off him. *'Don't you dare mess with my daughter!'* *'Don't you dare...'* The strict old man had repeated that phrase to *Skylar* over and over that day. And she hadn't, had she? She'd not dared deviate again from the path her father had set out for her. The narrow path of academic excellence, loyalty to the benefactor that was Helberg.

He got it. He really did. He'd wanted to protect his mother for years, suppressing the anger inside him because he couldn't be honest with her. He hadn't been able to tell her he didn't want to go to that damned school. Hadn't been able to tell her he was hurting. How badly he hurt for years with that injury—because he'd not wanted to make her feel worse. Because he'd not wanted to cause her more trouble.

As an adult he'd rationalised it all. He'd known his mother had been exhausted, working hard at two jobs— that she'd thought that scholarship would be best for him because she'd believed she couldn't meet his needs. But she'd not asked him if it were what he wanted. Equally, he'd not said.

And he'd been so alone for so long. Because he'd gone the opposite way to Skylar—he'd gone for hedonism. Using temporary pleasure to wash away the pain but keeping it short, meaningless, keeping himself safe. Anything more took too much *effort*.

Only it didn't take any effort with Skylar. So easily he could laugh with her. And he'd told her truths he'd barely been able to face himself. He could tease her and play sexy little games that he loved. Only with her.

Because it was *her*. He'd had such a crush on her back then. He'd wanted her so much. But he was completely in love with her now. Not that he'd told her. No. He'd turned his back on her. Because she scared the hell out of him.

He wasn't good enough, right? And hearing that again? *Losing* her? He couldn't tolerate that. Which was why he was here now, indulging in a futile attempt to wash away a hangover of epic proportions.

Maybe she had wanted to speak up for him that morning all those years ago, but she'd been too shocked, too scared. Hell, it had only been a moment—they'd hardly spoken. He'd been blown away by the intensity—maybe she had too. And she'd have been terrified of her father.

Zane had turned his back and walked—had to—stung by them both.

But Skylar had been stuck. Had to stay for so much more of the same. And she'd become such a people pleaser. She put everyone else first. *Everyone*. Her father. Her colleagues. A whole damn company. She'd not stopped to consider what it was *she* really wanted…she'd just stayed on that damn treadmill that she'd been set on because she thought she had to.

And she'd tried to please him too, hadn't she? Was it only because he'd plucked at her too-soft heartstrings in Bermuda—telling her about the accident?

No, it had been for so much longer than that. She'd barely known him at the beginning of the bet business because he kept all his cards close. But she'd known enough about him to be aware that he liked games. That he didn't want a *relationship*. So she'd, what, made a play that she thought he could tolerate?

But after Bermuda, when he'd ended their deal, she'd asked if they could keep seeing each other anyway. Then at the bar last night she'd suggested he needed people in his life. But she'd not expressly suggested herself. Had that been because she'd been afraid of asking outright—afraid of his rejection? Did she want something more with him?

Hope soared. Because *he* was the only man she'd ever

let touch her. She'd let *him* in. Actions, not words, right? And it wasn't solely about 'education.'

But while she'd played with him, while she'd been confident enough to take something of what she wanted, she'd still put *his* wishes ahead of her own.

She'd asked him if he was okay. She'd wanted him to say what he really felt…but he hadn't shared that part of himself with her. He'd not told her his truth. Because he still believed that he wasn't what she wanted, that he wasn't best for her. He'd assumed it was all only about Helberg for her. What if he'd been wrong about that?

Had she done exactly what he did? Had she hid her hurt—not admitted her feelings—not said what she really felt, or what *she* really wanted…?

And by staying silent, Zane hadn't let her make her own informed choice about their future. He'd made it for her by pushing her away. In all that assumption, he'd pushed her into the same place she'd been with her father.

Silenced.

He'd been selfish. And controlling. And yeah, a complete coward.

He growled, letting the icy water stream over his face. *Enough* of that already!

CHAPTER EIGHTEEN

THE DANCING PHASE lasted about forty minutes. She didn't want to dance with anyone but him. Didn't want to dance without him at all. Her feet hurt, her heart bled, her eyes watered. Infuriated, she went home and threw herself into work. That phase lasted about five minutes.

She didn't want to work like this any more. And, she accepted, she didn't *have* to.

She didn't get out of bed the next day. She slept. She thought. And yes, she cried. In her weakest moments she looked online. Zane's tally on that stupid website hadn't increased. It had stopped at two and there were no more pictures of him dining or dancing with another woman last night. But it was only a matter of time though, right?

Because it was over between them. He wasn't going to wake up and realise he was in love with her...the way she was in love with him.

Yeah, she could admit that now—to herself at least. And she'd sort of told him last night, in a tragically weird way, trying to convince him he needed someone in his life.

Of course she'd meant herself. And of course he'd stood like a stone.

But while he didn't feel the same, she couldn't believe what they'd shared was *nothing*. They had a real connection—more than their shared past, more than the undeniable sexual chemistry. He just didn't want it to last. And fine. But that didn't stop her holding her breath, hoping and wishing. Checking her phone. But no matter how long she stared at it, he didn't message her.

She couldn't—and wouldn't—wait for ever. *She* had to move forward too. But it would be in a different way to him. She'd worked so hard and been so loyal to everyone else *but* herself for too long. She'd not blossomed in all these years—she'd been blinkered.

She needed time away to figure out and focus on the things she *could* attain—*other* than Zane himself. And there was much—the travel she'd not done. She needed to explore all the other beaches, see all the other amazing buildings in the world. And she could—because she had money saved. All that money to buy her father a better house and she hadn't been able to because he'd passed too soon. All the money sitting there because shc'd not spoiled herself. Not gone anywhere.

Then there were the job opportunities she'd not explored—heck, maybe she'd go for a whole career change. She owed it to herself to reach for the life she wanted. The one she'd not taken true hold of... She could get excited about that. She could make something more for herself. And she would be okay.

She picked up her phone and adjusted some settings so there'd be no point in looking forlornly at it any more.

And on Monday morning it was time to move.

It was appallingly easy for them to accept her resignation. For her to gather the few personal things she had in her desk. She didn't even need a box. Then she got on the bus heading east, the route familiar and slow. She'd do her farewell tour.

And then she'd be free.

* * *

Zane waited at reception, his back turned to that portrait of Reed Helberg. Cleared his throat. Checked his watch. Adjusted his collar. Ignored the dagger looks the receptionist shot him every other interminable second. It was Bernie who finally appeared. Zane saw his face and was hit by a bad really feeling.

'Where is she?' Zane asked as soon as Bernie was within earshot.

She'd blocked his number. When he'd tried calling her from an alternate phone she still hadn't picked up. He'd gone to her apartment and she wasn't home. Not during the day. Not late at night. She wasn't around.

'She's finished up. Gone away.'

'Gone *where*?'

Surely not. It was only Tuesday. She wouldn't walk out on her job without giving due notice. That wasn't Skylar's way. But maybe she'd really wanted to get away.

While that was terrifying, it also fuelled him. Because it meant she was upset. And not all about her job.

The old guy looked at him with total disappointment in his eyes. 'I think she leaves the country in a couple of days.'

Zane had to take a moment. 'So where is she now? You really don't know?'

'No. I'm sorry.'

Zane believed him. Because while she considered these guys family, she didn't open up to them. It was like she was still shut away in her room upstairs, looking out the window at the world. Still lonely.

He spent an hour wondering where the one place she'd go before leaving the country for a while might be. And then it was obvious.

He drove himself—tearing back down the very road

he'd driven only the day before. Back to Belhaven Bay. He drove past the site where their old building complex had been. He went to the beach. He went to the cafe. It was only when he happened to drive past the cemetery on his way to their old school that he slammed on the brakes. He'd almost missed her sitting on that park bench in the middle of the memorial gardens.

He took in a couple of steadying breaths before getting out of the car. He had to be so careful. She wanted to travel and he refused to stand in the way of her doing something she really wanted for herself. But he didn't want her to leave without being honest with her. He owed her that. He owed himself too. So he would control himself here. But at least she would know she was loved. That she meant so very much to him.

And he would accept whatever happened.

She glanced up when he approached. Paled. Her hair was in a messy ponytail and her eyes red-rimmed.

'You've left Helberg,' he said.

'I have a lot of holidays owed so I was able to leave with immediate effect,' she said. 'I'm going to travel. Sit on some other beaches. Run at some other parks. Figure out what I really want in my future.'

He nodded. 'That sounds great.'

She stood but didn't move closer, just hesitated with her arms wrapped around her waist. 'What are you doing here?'

'I…uh… I wanted to tell you…' His throat was scratchy and he swallowed, finding it almost impossible to speak.

But she waited silently. He appreciated her patience. And he would make this effort. Always.

He cleared his throat. 'I was here over the weekend. Came late on Saturday night…' He'd run away and drowned his sorrows. It hadn't worked. 'That's not what I came here to tell you though.'

'No?'

'You're a loyal person, Skylar. You put other people first all the time. Their needs. You should dare to be free, Skylar. Dare to do whatever you want.'

She lost a little colour. 'You want me to be happy.'

'Yes.'

'You want me to do what *I* want.'

'Yes. Exactly.' His heart pounded. 'I want the best for you.'

She stared at him. 'Why?'

He was actually trembling inside. This beautiful woman who he'd wanted for so long, the woman he'd finally truly got to know. The woman he'd completely fallen for. Was standing in front of him and about to leave.

'You were right,' he coughed. 'I don't just hide hurt, Skylar. I hide all my feelings. And that's not fair of me.'

'Okay.'

He twisted up inside. 'That's just it. I'm not okay.'

Skylar could hold herself together for only so long. She didn't want to interrupt him—didn't want him to ever stop talking in that gentle way—but at the same time she couldn't stand to see him. He was heartbreakingly gorgeous.

'I'm not okay,' he whispered again. 'Not without you.'

The echo of her pulse in her eardrums was deafening. She willed him to say more. Or to move—to step forward and pull her into his arms. She would take that. She would take anything.

But he suddenly covered his face with his hands. 'I'm so scared of having you and losing you. I want you so much.

In my life. Always. But I don't want to—' He broke off and looked skywards and swore. 'I'm screwing this up, Skylar.'

'Why are you here?'

He drew in a harsh breath. 'I don't want to confuse you. I don't want to stand in your way. I don't want to hold you back from anything, ever. I don't want to say this and have it have any sway over your decisions because that's what you do for the people in your life... But also, I think I have to say this, Skylar.'

So many things he didn't want if he... 'Say what?'

His hands dropped. 'I love you.'

'What?' She stared at him, not wanting to move or breathe. She just wanted a replay of what he'd just said. Had he said—

'I ended our agreement after Bermuda because I was uncomfortable. I know we strike sparks when we get within ten feet of each other, but I need you to know that this became so much more than that for me. More than some fun game. More than unfinished business from a lifetime ago.'

'How much more?'

'Everything more.' He remained frozen, so far away. 'That's what I meant by "I love you." Like completely, utterly, totally, I am in love with you.'

She had to put her hand on the back of the park bench for balance. 'You what?'

'It's you, it's always been you.'

'But—'

'I know there've been other women.' He looked awkward. 'And I know it sounds bad, but none of them meant anything much.'

She understood, actually. 'You didn't let them get near enough to matter.'

Because this brilliant, strong, kind man didn't think

he was worthy of someone—his father had left him, his mother had struggled to cope with him alone, he'd been rejected by the most powerful man in town, and he'd been crushed—literally. So he'd suppressed so much. His pain. His needs. He'd rebuilt himself—but there was still that little bit broken inside.

'You matter,' he said softly. 'Always have. I watched you…you came back from that school and you were different.'

A smile escaped. 'You mean I'd been through puberty?'

He chuckled softly. 'Not just that, you were so…serene and focused and I wanted to talk to you. I should have talked to you. But I got near and…' He lifted his shoulders.

They were on that runaway train together.

'And you don't think *you're* the best thing ever to walk back into my life?'

His pale blue eyes widened.

He'd been a handful of a boy. He was a handful of a man. And she loved him for it. Because he was gold—through and through.

'I mean it,' she said. 'I know I'm a pleaser. I want people to like me—to need me—that's true. But I could be me around you. Free. Maybe at the start I thought it didn't matter because it was only a game, but now it matters more than anything. *You* matter more than anything,' she whispered. 'And I'm so, so sorry.'

'Why?' He paled. 'For what? What are—'

'I should have said something that day Dad caught us. I just stood there and let him berate you, let him chase you off, let him think you were pushy when I should have spoken up and stopped him.'

'Oh.' He released a massive sigh. 'No.' He shook his head

gently. 'We both did what we had to, to be safe. In here.' He pressed his hand to his chest. 'I don't blame you for that.'

'But I hurt you.' She realised it now.

So had her dad. He'd made him feel unworthy. It had been another blow in that pile-on he'd felt.

His shoulders lifted. 'You were hurt too. And, sweetheart, we were kids.' He smiled sadly. 'Far too young to be able to handle something this big.'

Skylar trembled. This was that big for him too? Overwhelming and all-encompassing and wonderful…and terrifying. But now he was here. He'd come after her.

'You came to see him?' Zane gestured towards her father's grave.

'To tell him I've left Helberg.' She nodded and gazed at her father's small headstone. 'You know he never dated anyone or anything after my mother left. He was so self-contained and he encouraged me to be the same—that just the two of us was all we needed. I guess he thought it was safe.' She looked back up at Zane and saw the intensity in his eyes.

'He didn't think I was good enough for you,' he muttered.

'In his view, *no one* would have been good enough for me,' she said. 'But it wasn't his choice.'

She drank in Zane's stance—he was so focused on her. He listened. He cared. He loved her. And she needed to make him understand that she loved him right back. So much.

Emboldened, she stepped closer to him. 'This is *my* life and my choice. And I don't want to be alone.'

Zane's eyes flashed.

'I want a relationship, not a fling.' Her voice both rose

and shook. 'I want one love for a lifetime. I want a home. And I want a family. Children. And a dog. Two, actually.'

'What else?' he muttered huskily.

'I want to travel and see all the things I've not seen yet.' She blinked but through the tears she saw he'd stepped closer still.

'Sounds amazing. Is there more? What else do you want?'

Blinking again, she saw the vitality just bursting from him—his expression both light and hard and so very focused. Her courage overflowed, because his feelings were undeniable and so very obvious.

'*You,*' she said simply. 'With me. I want us to do it all together.'

'I would love to. I would love to do all that with you, Skylar.' He opened his arms and she just toppled into them.

'All that. All that and so much more.' He caught and held her tightly. 'But I don't want to stop you discovering everything else you want. I don't want to cramp your style—'

'You could *never.* You're the one who encourages me into some really creative things.' Her teary laugh was muffled against his chest. 'I want you *with* me.'

'Okay then.'

She felt his deep sigh.

'Always,' he whispered.

Yeah. That's what she wanted.

Drawing back but still holding Zane's hand tightly, she turned to face her father's grave. 'I love you, Daddy,' she whispered. 'And I know you loved me and I know you wanted to keep me safe. But I know you were hurt and you worried a little too much and held me a little too tight.' She told him what she'd been too young and too scared to say so long ago. 'But Zane's a good man. I love him and he loves me and we're going to be okay.' She drew in a shaky breath. 'We're going to have it all.'

Zane didn't let go of her hand the entire car ride—releasing her only to get out of the car and round to her door. Then he wrapped his arm around her waist and led her into the house, up the stairs, straight to his bedroom.

'I love you,' he said before she could breathe. 'I love you.'

He kissed her and told her over and over. She had no idea how they got naked, how they got into the bed. All she knew was that they were together—naked and entwined, and he was loving her with his words and his body and his spirit. And he was hers—really and truly hers.

Hours later, she stood wrapped in the top sheet, looking out at the stunning view of the garden and the beach beyond. 'I love it here,' she breathed.

He wound his arm around her from behind. 'Plenty of room for our kids and the dogs to roam free, don't you think? We can watch them playing from the balcony up here.'

She nodded, leaning back against him. 'That would make this great view unbeatable.'

'Yeah.'

And that was exactly what it did.

CHAPTER NINETEEN

Three years later

DANIELLE CHAPMAN'S ANNUAL Fourth of July party was in full swing. The beat of music and the bubble of chatter wafted through the still summer night, easily reaching the ears of the woman lying on the sun lounger that was artfully placed beneath an old cherry tree, hidden by the thick hedge that formed the boundary between the two vast beachfront properties.

Skylar wasn't wearing white, because she wasn't going to the party at all—she was in a scarlet bikini and, despite the rapid approach of dusk, she was still feeling hot. She was also feeling huge. She heard the clink of ice and glanced up to see her husband walking towards her balancing two tall glasses of she didn't know what, but she knew it would be delicious.

Actually, it was her bare-chested husband who was delicious. Clad only in beach shorts and sandals, every muscle was on display. She felt hotter still.

'Something you need, Skylar?' Zane chuckled and set the glasses down on the small table that had been dragged near the lounger long ago.

'You know me too well,' she muttered.

He ran a fingertip over her lower lip. 'Pregnancy makes you very hungry.'

'It does,' she purred. 'I need a *lot* of attention.'

This was their favourite place to be alone together. Where they'd spent many lazy summer afternoons, dozing, reading, making love...

The first year they'd travelled lots. They'd both walked away from Helberg, but Skylar had been beyond touched to learn Zane had offered Bernie and the other older employees a guarantee on their Helberg investment in case things went bad. Bernie had since retired, his pension fund intact.

Zane had cut back on the hours he'd worked and reprioritised. They'd married in this very garden only a few months in—the two of them standing in the trees with only Danielle as witness. Danielle who'd been astounded and then enchanted to learn of their history and delighted to be part of their very private celebration.

At the end of that first year, Skylar had discovered she was pregnant. They'd not been trying, but they'd not been *not* trying...and it had happened quicker than either of them had imagined it would. They'd been ecstatic. Eight months later her impatient son had arrived. He had his father's eyes and demanding nature and she adored him.

Right now he was inside their home cuddled up with the puppy, being read to by his doting grandmother, who was tasked with keeping him awake just long enough to catch a glimpse of the fireworks from Danielle's party.

Zane had asked Skylar to come with him to visit his mother not long after that day by her father's grave. It had been awkward between mother and son at first. Skylar had chattered to fill the gaps, but slowly things had got easier and both Zane and his mother had talked through some of the tough times in their past. She'd finally retired and even let Zane help her. Now she visited often. It gave Zane no end of pleasure to see his mother relaxed and able to enjoy spending time with their small, inquisitive boy. They were all looking forward to the arrival of his little sister—due in four months' time.

'What attention would you *particularly* like?' Zane rested his hands either side of her and bent over her.

She just wanted all of him. Now. She curled her arms around his neck and tugged him so he toppled down to her.

'Careful,' he grunted. 'I don't want to crush you.'

She slipped from beneath him, giving him a nudge so he rolled onto his back. In seconds she straddled him and greedily worked the waistband of his shorts down. But he was busy too. He released her hair from its ponytail first— as he so often liked to do. Then he tugged the strings of her bikini top until they became dangerously loose, but didn't go further.

'Are you playing with me?' she asked archly as she teased him every bit as much.

'Is this a game?' He batted his lashes wickedly. 'Or is this a *race*?'

'Oh, it's a game,' she whispered.

'No, it's a race,' he whispered right back before snatching the bikini from her and cupping her breasts in both hands.

She shuddered as his thumbs teased her sensitive tips. But she shook her head and worked her hands that bit harder.

'I like watching you come first,' he growled. 'Then I like watching you come again.'

'Come *with* me or I'll turn my back and then you won't see my face.'

His wicked smile broadened and he swept his hands over

her belly and below. 'Reverse cowgirl is always acceptable,' he drawled. 'I can touch you where you like it most. And I love it when you scream and whip your hair in my face.'

She flushed and giggled at the same time. Next second she gasped. *'Zane!'*

He felled her. Every time. He rose up and wrapped his arms around her to hold her close, kissing her as he finally filled her and succumbed to the sparks between them. She clung, quivering as she welcomed him back to her heart. They moved fast yet gentle—playful and passionate—until they were out of control and shaking in ecstasy together.

'I love you,' he panted.

This was the race he liked to win—to say it first in the mornings, to say it the most. To mean it always.

But it was no game really. Skylar held his handsome face in her hands and gazed right into his eyes. 'I love you too.'

His smile was stunning—so satisfied and smug and yet full of wonder that she'd said it still. They'd given each other the family they both craved. The security they both needed. All the love they'd secretly longed for. And it all just kept growing.

She kissed him. Fireworks whistled and burst above them, filling the sky with sound and colour before fading all too quickly.

But Zane and Skylar made their own fireworks. And they always would.

* * * * *